Love Lives On

Sidney W. Frost

Published by Sidney W. Frost
153 Cattle Trail Way
Georgetown, TX 78633
sidfrost@suddenlink.net
http://sidneywfrost.com

Printed in the United States by CreateSpace.com

Editor: Lisa Lickel
Book cover design by Sidney W. Frost

Cover photos:
    Bruges, Belgium: © Sidney W. Frost
    Woman: © Yuri Arcurs I Dreamstime.com

ISBN: 0-9830708-4-9
ISBN-13: 978-0-9830708-4-9

DEDICATION

This book is dedicated to
bookmobile librarians and drivers
around the world.

CHAPTER ONE

Karen Williams was fifty-four and divorced for so long she'd given up hope for that special marriage everyone talked about, but few probably had experienced. Then, a year ago, her life changed. Her college sweetheart charged back into her life, acting as if he'd never stopped loving her. He was waiting for her at the altar now as she touched up her makeup in the bride's room of her church.

She hurried to apply mascara, but her right hand wouldn't be still. The pencil hit the table with a soft clunk. Tears followed. Tears from nowhere. A glance into the mirror showed mascara running down both cheeks. What was happening?

Was it that feeling of unworthiness that crept in when she least expected it? Couldn't be. God had forgiven her long ago, but she would never forget what had happened. Second thoughts? Definitely not. She loved Brian and he loved her. He would never do anything to hurt her. Not again.

***

Brian Donelson looked at his watch again. She was now officially late. The buzz in the congregation meant he wasn't the only one who sensed something was wrong. All his friends and Karen's friends were laughing softly, but he knew there was no reason to be concerned. Not yet. Surely she'd walk up the aisle in a few minutes.

Perhaps he should announce a delay. Ardis Twiss stared at him from her perch on the organ bench as if asking what to do. He shrugged and she kept playing.

All the turmoil he'd endured the past thirty years came back to him now. His sin. His self-loathing. His unhappiness with his life. He accepted that God had forgiven him for what he'd done, so why was he thinking about it now? He feared she'd changed her mind about marrying him.

Phil was all decked out in a tux with his gray hair complementing his caramel-colored skin. He took his best man duties seriously. He whispered to the pastor, just loud enough for Brian to hear, "We're checking on the bride." He then gave Brian a questioning look.

Pastor Jim Dunlap merely nodded and waited patiently. He didn't seem flustered at all. Maybe this was nothing new to him.

Brian had a sudden image of Karen driving away from the church with a corner of her long white wedding gown sticking out from under the driver's side door. He remembered she'd told him she wasn't wearing a traditional bridal gown. His imagination adjusted to show her in a suit, but still in her car speeding away from the church. He saw himself running after the car holding the bride's bouquet high in the air, yelling to her that she'd forgotten to get married so she could toss the flowers to all the single women. His legs were like rubber as he moved them faster and faster without going forward.

He took in a deep breath, tested his legs, and shook his head to erase the vision. Could their relationship survive one more difficulty? He hoped so.

***

Karen was glad she'd picked a dress she could wear again instead of a bridal gown. She'd worn a long white one when she married Steve only to have their marriage end in divorce.

"Well, is there going to be a wedding today, or not?" The question came from a large, some say full-figured, woman standing in the doorway. The floral dress she wore wasn't much different from her everyday attire at the library, but it appeared to be newer.

"I'm glad you're here, Liz," Karen said, standing. "I need your help."

Karen knew Liz was a hugger. Still, she was caught off guard when Liz put her arms around her and held her tight.

"What can I do, darlin'?" Liz asked as she let go of Karen and moved back to look into her eyes.

Karen's hands quivered ever so slightly as she gripped them together in front of her chest. "I need to talk to Brian."

That was all it took. No questions asked. Liz was heading out the door when she called back over her shoulder, "I'll get him."

He entered the room soon afterwards.

"Oh, Brian. I'm sorry for holding up the wedding, but I have to tell you something."

"What?"

"First, let me say I love you deeply and I hope what I have to say doesn't change your mind about marrying me."

"Nothing could do that," he said.

"Don't be so quick to answer. Remember all the little and not so little surprises we had for each other during the past year? Well, this is one I wanted to tell you. I just didn't know how to say it."

"You don't have to tell me if you don't want to. It doesn't make a difference to me. I love you and want to marry you. No matter what."

She smiled and hugged him. "I'm glad you feel that way. But, after so many years of keeping this secret, I didn't know what to do."

"Why are you bringing it up now?"

She gazed at those eyes she loved so much and kissed him. "Because I told you there were no more secrets."

Brian smiled as he took her in his arms and held her close. "That's all? No problem. Let's get married." He kissed her back. "Of course I want to hear all about it later. Okay?"

They turned and left the room, walking hand in hand down the hall toward the sanctuary.

***

Phil's father George was the only one ready to go when Karen and Brian got to the narthex. Brian's daughter Amy was talking on the phone while her own daughter Julie played some game on her smart phone. Karen's best friend Cathy was stretched out on the couch with her eyes closed. George stood at attention at the door to the church waiting to walk Karen down the aisle and give her away.

He turned to the bridal party. "Let's go, ladies. It's show time."

The three women came over of hugged Karen and got in line to walk down the aisle.

Brian handed Karen's arm to George in a gesture for him to take it from there. "I guess I better get back to the altar before everyone leaves," Brian said.

"Not to worry," George said. "No one left. Ever'body wants to know how this soap opera's goin' to turn out."

Brian smiled. "Everything is just fine."

Karen nodded.

Brian walked down the hallway on the right side of the sanctuary to reach the altar while Karen looked into the church from the narthex. The organ music was nearly drowned out by the many voices all talking at once. The buzz from multiple conversations died down when someone noticed Brian was back and asked loud enough for all to hear, "Did you find her?"

Everyone chuckled as Brian smiled and gave a thumbs up. A rippling of applause began and quickly grew to a roaring accolade as he moved in next to Phil. Ardis sat up straighter on her bench and started shuffling the music on the stand.

Karen pulled George closer. "I think you're right. Everyone's here, and they're pulling for us."

"Amen," he said. "Ever'body here loves you two and wants you to be happy."

The music started softly as the bridal party walked down the aisle, but the volume quickly increased. Soon everyone was quiet and on their feet looking toward the entrance where Karen and George stood. Two photographers stepped into the aisle between them and the front of the church. One was the woman Karen hired and the other was a young man she'd never seen before. They both snapped photos then jumped out of the way.

When Karen and George reached the altar, the pastor asked, "Who gives this woman to be married to this man?"

George was resplendent in his tux. His glasses sat so low on his nose he gazed out over the top of the wire rims. His curly black hair speckled with gray glistened from perspiration or hair oil. As usual he stood erect with his head held high. Today, though, when the pastor asked who gave this woman, he seemed taller. "I do," he said in his booming voice as he handed Karen to Brian.

She smiled as she moved into the position next to her fiancé and prepared to take her vows. Her mind stayed on the unknown photographer and the doubts she couldn't explain. When she faced the congregation she turned toward George and mouthed a "thank you." Her father walked her down the aisle when she'd married Steve, but both he and her mother died a few years ago. They would have loved Brian and been pleased she was marrying him.

The room was silent as George returned to his seat. Karen nodded at Phil who stood next to Brian.

"Who is that young photographer?" she whispered to Brian.

He looked around then shrugged.

Pastor Jim focused on Karen. "Is everything okay?" he asked, speaking softly.

"Yes. Sorry for holding up the ceremony."

He didn't seem upset that she'd kept him waiting. Standing here in front of her friends reminded her what a huge step they were taking. She took a few breaths to calm her body. Brian squeezed her hand. Was he nervous, too? Probably. He blinked more than usual and his forehead was covered with perspiration.

"Brian, face Karen and hold her right hand in yours," the pastor said. After a pause and in a voice all could hear, he continued. "Now, repeat after me."

She saw only Brian.

"In the name of God, I, Brian, take you, Karen, to be my wife, to have and to hold from this day forward, for better for worse, for richer, for poorer, in sickness and in health, to love and to cherish, until we are parted by death. This is my solemn vow."

After they both repeated their vows, the pastor nodded to Phil and Cathy for the rings. "Bless, O Lord, these rings to be a sign of the vows by which this man and this woman have bound themselves to each other. Through Jesus Christ our Lord. Amen."

They placed the rings on one another saying, "I give you this ring as a symbol of my vow, and with all that I am, and all that I have, I honor you, in the Name of God."

The pastor joined their right hands and said, "Now that Karen and Brian have given themselves to each other by solemn vows, with the joining of hands and the giving and receiving of rings, I pronounce that they are husband and wife, in the Name of the Father, and of the Son, and of the Holy Spirit. Those whom God has joined together let no one put asunder."

When the ceremony ended and they turned to be introduced to their friends as Mr. and Mrs. Donelson, Karen saw more than friends. Another unknown person stood on the side of the sanctuary, staring at her. He seemed angry with his arms crossed. She should acknowledge those happy faces in the crowd, but she couldn't take her eyes off the frowning one. As they walked down the aisle, she scanned the area for other strangers. She didn't see one until they reached the narthex. The young photographer pushed his way past the woman Karen had hired.

Brian went with the pastor to sign papers while Karen hung back with the photographers. The same negative feeling she'd experienced before the wedding came over her again as a man she didn't recognize approached her.

"Karen Williams Donelson?" he asked.

"Yes."

"I'm sorry to bother you at this occasion, but I must give you this." He handed her an envelope.

She took it, holding it away from her body as if it could harm her. "Who are you? What is this?"

"Ma'am, you're being sued. I don't know why. I only deliver the papers. Like I said, I'm sorry."

"Sued? Who's suing me?"

"I don't know that either, ma'am. You'll find all that information in the envelope." He nodded and turned around to leave. Before he got far, Liz had him by the arm and walked him to the exit.

Brian returned and stood by Karen's side. "Who was that?" he asked.

She held the envelope for him see. "A process server, I guess. He gave me this. Said I'm being sued."

She pulled out the document and scanned it quickly before returning it to its envelope. "We'll look at this later," she said, holding the envelope next to her hip. "Right now all I want to think about is our wedding day."

The rest of the wedding party moved in closer after the stranger was escorted out. Karen held Brian tightly and smiled at their friends. Still, she couldn't help wonder about what she had seen in the envelope.

CHAPTER TWO

The reception was held at the cabin, the getaway Brian had built up the hill from his home on Dry Creek near Lake Austin. *Their* home now.

Brian tried to relax and enjoy what he could of the day—a day he'd waited so long for. But he couldn't celebrate until he found out who was suing Karen and why. He needed to be with her at this time, not playing host at a party.

If only they'd gotten married thirty years ago when they should have. They wouldn't be facing lawsuits or worrying about getting all the secrets out on the table. They'd have their own children, together, and maybe a grandchild or two. It could've been.

He looked around the cabin for Karen and spotted his daughter talking to Karen's daughter. Seeing Amy and Julie reminded him nothing would be the same if they had married back then.

He'd had the cabin built on the exact spot of the one the Combine rented while in college some thirty odd years ago. The six guys, Brian, Phil, Ron, Tony, Richard, and Matt, called themselves the Combine while in college and the name stuck, as did the friendships. Richard was the one they needed to talk to now. He was an attorney who practiced family law.

Brian built the new cabin to match the outer appearance of the original, but it was more spacious and much more well-appointed. When they were students at the University of Texas, the six of them had to scrape and save to come up with the rent each month. Money was no longer a problem for them and Brian bought the property last year for mostly nostalgic reasons. Now the Combine got together there after dining out each month.

As Brian moved around the large room talking to guests, he learned the wedding itself, that is, the vows and promises part, seemed boring compared to the events leading up to the time when Karen got there. Everyone had debated about whether or not she would show. It was all in good fun, so Brian let them all know how he'd feared the worst, in a joking way, of course. Most of the guests hadn't noticed the process server, and those who had, didn't know why he was there.

It wasn't long before the Combine surrounded Brian. They would have questions.

Richard went first. "You're not going to tell us why Karen was late to the altar, are you? Come on, give us something. Tony said it had to be a costume malfunction. The rest of us thought she'd changed her mind and you had to go talk her into marrying you all over again."

"Yeah, man," Phil said. "What happened?"

"Tell us," Ron said.

Even though the questions caused his heart rate to rise, Brian smiled. Having your bride warn you she had one more secret to tell just minutes before you tied the knot was one thing. But having that topped off with a process server showing up was more than most new grooms could stand. He wanted to tell everyone to leave so he could talk to his wife and find out what was going on.

Brian pulled in close to his friends. "Listen, guys. Just trust me. There's nothing serious going on. I'll tell you what I can, but I don't know much yet." He paused while looking at each one separately before focusing on Richard. "We need to talk to you...can you hang around a few minutes after everyone leaves?"

"Sure...as a friend, or as your attorney?"

"Both."

The rest of the guys eased up after hearing what Brian had said to Richard.

"Changing subjects," Ron said, "why didn't you tell us Liz has a boyfriend?"

"Boyfriend? First I've heard anything about it. Are you sure?"

"Yeah," Tony said. "She introduced him as her new friend, but I could tell she meant boyfriend. Name's Virgil something."

"She didn't say anything to me about it," Brian said. "I think it's great, though." He looked around the room. "Well, I better go see how Karen's doing. Thanks for understanding, guys."

He walked toward the clump of women, mostly Combine wives, surrounding Karen.

Before he reached her, Liz grabbed his arm. "Oh, there you are," she said, with pastor Jim standing next to her. "I told the preacher about the cabin and he asked a question I couldn't answer."

Brian flushed. One bit of history Liz didn't know was that he and Karen had first made love in the original cabin.

They were different people now. This time they had decided to wait until marriage to consummate their vows.

The pastor cleared his voice. "I asked Liz if the house was here when you and your friends rented the cabin."

"No. The original cabin was behind the Dry Creek Saloon and there were no other buildings in the area. We stumbled on the for rent sign one day driving back from Mount Bonnell and started renting it as a place to get away from home. We all lived with our parents at the time and, for ten dollars a month, the cabin gave us an independence none of us had experienced."

"Ten dollars?" the pastor asked.

"Well, there were six of us, and the rent was sixty dollars a month. You've got to remember this was thirty years ago and, quite frankly, some of us had trouble finding that extra ten bucks each month. It wasn't big enough for us to live in. And there was only one small bedroom. But it was great for us to pretend we were grown. Some of us actually studied here and of course we'd have the occasional party."

"Do you and Karen plan to stay here?" the pastor asked.

"Yes. As long as Karen likes it. One nice thing is that there's room enough to park the bookmobile here. "

The pastor raised his eyebrows. "Bookmobile?"

"That's another story," Brian said. "Liz can explain it. I need to check on Karen."

"That's okay. Rita and I should be leaving, anyway. We'll learn about the bookmobile later. I just want to thank you for inviting us."

"You're welcome," Brian said. "Thank you for marrying us."

After the pastor and his wife had left, Brian turned to Liz. "I need to talk to Karen."

"Go. I understand. Later, you're going to tell me why she held up the wedding so long and what that little hullaballoo in the narthex was all about at the end of the service."

He would, too. Liz had a special knack for pulling the most personal information from people.

He saw Karen talking to Julie and Amy. He smiled. Their daughters had become as close as sisters. He walked toward them, thinking how lucky he was to have three beautiful women in his life. Both the girls were going to the University of Texas. Julie just beginning her studies to be a teacher and Amy working on an MBA.

Brian continued his mission to reach Karen, and when he got there he took her into an embrace and nuzzled her face, causing Julie and Amy to groan in unison and walk away. "I'm thinking about announcing the end of this party so we can have some privacy. Sound okay?" Brian asked, as he kissed her behind the ear.

She smiled at him mischievously, eyebrows raised. "As much as I enjoy being alone with you, not yet. These people stood by us through all our ups and downs." She paused and looked around the room. "Many of them knew this day would come before either of us did."

He put his arms around her. "I know. Besides, we wouldn't be alone. I asked Richard to stay so we can talk to him about the lawsuit."

"I hoped you would. But we have an obligation to stay here and talk to our friends more. It won't be long, okay?"

He'd notice her quiver when he mentioned the lawsuit. She was right about the need to be with their friends, but was she stalling about the conversation they were going to have? What did she know about the papers? Was she worried about what Richard would say? What had she tried to tell him before the wedding?

Nothing she could say would change his love for her. Brian may have given up on marrying Karen a few times in the past year, but their friends never had. He hugged her again. "Okay. I get the point. As long as you're happy. Just know, I want you. And soon."

"I know," she said, pulling him closer. "Me too. I'm making the rounds, but I haven't talked to everyone yet."

Brian kissed her on the cheek. "If you have too much of this, just say the word and I'll clear the room." Brian couldn't help but think about getting alone with his wife. Was that what was driving his concern for her? He didn't think so. He wasn't in a hurry, he had the rest of his life to love her. Still, each time he kissed her or held her close, he was reminded of what could be. He kissed her again, this time on the cheek.

When people started saying their good byes and leaving, Brian didn't try to change minds. He and Karen stood at the door and shook the hands of their guests as they departed.

When they thought everyone was gone, they turned around and saw a small army cleaning up in the kitchen area, Richard included. If they could get everyone else to leave, they could talk to him about the lawsuit. After that conversation, they could finally be alone and go to bed. Thirty years was a long time to wait to be with the one he'd always loved.

"Look," he said to Karen. "We've got help."

"Good," Karen said. "Since we're leaving for our honeymoon tomorrow, we should clean up before we go."

"Hey," Cathy hollered across the room, "are you two going to help or not?"

Brian and Karen walked quickly over to where Cathy, Julie, and Amy were working. Matt and Richard and their wives were picking up and carrying empty plates to the kitchen while others loaded the dishwasher. Cathy's husband, Dudley, found the TV remote and stretched out in front of the screen watching a show.

"Hey, Mom," Julie said as she held the envelope the process server had delivered. "What's this?"

Karen turned to Brian. She'd placed the envelope in a cupboard when they first got there. She held out her hand to Julie. "Oh, it's nothing." She took the envelope, holding it by two fingers as if it were on fire. Brian took it and stuffed it into the breast pocket of his tux.

CHAPTER THREE

"Let's help clean up," Karen said to Brian. "We have a plane to catch in the morning."

"Too late," Liz said. "All the work is done. Just need to turn off a few lights and go home."

"Thank you, Liz," Karen said. "Thank you all."

"Yes," Brian said. "Thanks so much." He turned to Liz. "Where's Virgil? I haven't met him yet."

She blushed. "Oh, he's probably outside, smoking. Come, I'll introduce you."

Karen and Brian followed Liz to the door, but just as they got there, a tall slender man with long wavy black hair entered. The smell of cigarette smoke preceded him. His dark black suit was a stark contrast to Liz's wrinkled dress.

Liz grabbed his hand and turned toward Karen and Brian. "This is Virgil Golden. You've met Karen, of course, and this is her new husband, Brian, who worked with me on the bookmobile for about a year before I got promoted."

Virgil bowed to Karen. "I certainly have met the charming bride," he said with a fake English accent.

He took Brian's hand. "So nice to meet the groom as well."

Liz focused on her gentleman friend. "Karen and Brian drive the bookmobile now." She turned to Karen. "Virgil helps me at the library so you'll probably run into him there sometime."

"Nice to meet you," Brian said.

"Oh, by the way," Liz said to Karen, "I am so glad you agreed to work on the bookmobile with Brian. It's wonderful of him to provide the vehicle until we can get our own. But to drive it and provide a librarian, too. That's extra special."

"Thank you," Karen said. "I've enjoyed it."

Liz, Virgil, and the rest of the cleaning crew said good bye and moved toward the door.

"Dudley, turn off that TV," Cathy called. "We're leaving."

"Could you stay a few minutes?" Karen asked Cathy.

"Huh? Sure. What is it, that little gift you got at the end of the service?"

"Yes."

"Sit down, Dudley. We're not going yet."

Matt and his wife left. Karen asked Julie and Amy to stay also. Richard didn't have to be asked again. His wife, Linda, joined Dudley in the TV corner.

Karen held out a hand to Brian who pulled the envelope out of his pocket and gave it to her.

"I only got a quick look at the document, but I saw enough to know it has to do with Ernest."

"Who's Ernest?" Julie looked puzzled.

"Goodness sakes," Cathy's eyes grew large. "Ernest Brower," she said. "You told me never to mention his name again and here I am blurting it out at your wedding reception."

Julie looked at Amy and shrugged. "Who are you talking about?" she asked again.

Karen took her nineteen-year-old daughter's hand. "I'm sorry. I never told you about my first husband." Karen turned to Brian. "And I'm sorry I didn't tell you either."

"Was that what you wanted to say before the wedding?"

She nodded, searching his eyes for understanding.

"It wasn't a real marriage," Cathy said. "It was a marriage of convenience."

"A what?" Julie asked.

"Oh, you mean, to give him citizenship?" Amy asked.

Karen shook her head. "No, nothing like that. He had cancer and was terminal. He'd been a pillar in the church for many years, but by the time he became ill, there was no one to help. He'd lost his job and his home and would have had to take whatever care the government would provide. I had an excellent insurance plan and he had nothing. The only solution was to marry him and that's what I did."

Julie and Amy glanced at each other quickly before they moved in unison to Karen and placed their arms around her.

"Oh, Mom," Julie said. "That's nothing to be ashamed of."

"Right," Amy said. "You did a good thing, helping him like that."

Karen savored the love of her daughter and stepdaughter. Brian's eyes were clouded over. Was he happy or sad? Did he love her? Did he understand? Would he run off like he threatened to do last time the tension between them grew too strong? Every emotion in her body cried out and she knew she wanted Brian to stay with her for the rest of her life. She kissed each daughter on the cheek then moved to Brian.

She faced him and took one hand in each of hers. "Yes. This is what I wanted to tell you before the ceremony. The last secret. I promise. Can you stand being my third husband?"

The glaze on his eyes turned into tears. "Of course I can. As long as I'm your last husband, it doesn't matter."

Cathy turned toward Karen. "See, we didn't need to keep it a secret after all."

"Cathy's right," said Amy. "It's nothing like the way my mother tricked Dad into marrying her by telling him she was pregnant with me."

"Except," Karen said, "I told him there were no more skeletons in my closet."

Julie placed a hand on Karen's arm. "Mom, don't worry about it now. He understands. We all do."

"Thank you, girls," Karen said. She hugged Brian while holding the envelope tightly in her right hand. "And thank you."

She gave Richard the envelope she'd received from the process server. "Here."

Richard took the document out and flipped through the pages, stopping at times, reading without comment.

When he got to the last page, he turned toward Karen. "So Ernest was your first husband? Before Julie's father...what was his name?"

"Steve."

"Why don't you start at the beginning and tell us about Ernest," Richard said to Karen.

"Okay." She paused, wondering where to start. "I met Ernest when I was twenty-nine and had just started my teaching career after getting my master's degree from the University of Texas. Ernest was highly respected at our church. Older than me by thirty years or so. Divorced. Sunday school teacher. Loved by the congregation. We dated off and on. Nothing serious."

She paused again, wishing she didn't have to remember. "When he got sick and I found out he was broke, I had to do something. He had no family, no money, and no hope. I offered to help and he accepted. We got married so he could use my medical insurance.

Not that it could save his life, but it let him die with dignity."

She walked to the dining table, pulled out a chair and sat. Brian sat across from her while Richard took the chair next to Brian. Cathy reached for the chair next to Karen when Julie placed her hand on Cathy's shoulder.

"I think we should leave the two of them alone with Richard to talk about this," Julie said, looking at Cathy, then Amy. "Don't y'all agree?"

"Yes," Cathy said. She kissed Karen on the cheek. "But all you need to do is holler if you want me to do anything. Okay?"

"Yes, Cathy. Thank you."

"Come on Dudley," Cathy called out. "We're going home."

Julie and Amy both hugged Brian and Karen, preparing to leave.

Amy hesitated. "Since we're getting everything out in the open, I need to tell you Mom is threatening to sue for more alimony again," she said. "I suspect she's just blowing off steam, but I wanted you to know, just in case."

Brian gave Amy a peck on the cheek. "Thank you for the warning. It'll be okay."

"Yes, it will," Karen said.

Brian had provided a large settlement for his ex-wife, Judy, and successfully fought off her last attempt to get more.

"Tell us what happened next," Richard said.

Karen stared at the ceiling for a second before continuing her tale. "Ernest had lost his business because of his illness. Next, his house went back to the bank. He didn't tell me until afterwards. I don't know if I could have done anything about it or not, but it was a surprise. I let him move in with me. Besides needing a place to live, it would look better to the insurance company. What started out as a sham marriage began to look like a real one, even though I didn't plan for it to. We lived in separate bedrooms, just friends at first. But, even with his illness, he had this charisma that was so powerful I soon fell for him. Maybe it was a proximity thing, I'm not sure, but one day, without so much as a word spoken about it, we began to act like a real husband and wife."

What did Brian think of her now?

"You were married," he said as he raised his head answering her unasked question.

Karen went on with her story without responding to Brian's comment. "Then one day he tells me about Cloris Parker."

"Who's that?" Brian asked.

Richard flipped through the papers sitting in front of him on the table. "She's one of the plaintiffs in the case. She was married to Ernest."

"Right," Karen said. "She was Ernest's second wife. Few people at church realized they had been married. I didn't. I learned later that he married her because of the child."

Anger crept into Karen's body as she spoke. She wanted to be calm as she told her story, but she was far from it. She didn't try to hide her feelings from Brian or Richard, and wondered if she could if she wanted to.

"Now I understand," Brian said. "You took him in, gave him a home, supported him, and...loved him, and then, what? Did he still love Cloris?"

A tear rolled down her cheek as she looked at Brian and nodded. "Maybe it was because of the child, but Ernest was drawn to Cloris more than he was to me."

Brian handed her his handkerchief and she dabbed at her face. It was an unusual conversation on one's wedding night.

"Remember when I got sued last year," Brian said. "All my bank accounts were frozen for months until the case was dropped."

"I remember," Karen said. "You were going to run off to Germany."

Richard laughed. "I remember that, too."

Brian shook his head. "I'm sure glad that didn't happen. But this, being served on your wedding day...this is too much. I just wish I'd known to have guards at the door so he couldn't get in."

Karen patted Brian's arm. "It's not his fault. He was just doing his job."

"Yeah, but there was no need to serve the papers at the church."

"We're leaving for Germany tomorrow," Karen said. "Maybe that's why he did it today." She pointed to the documents in Richard's hands. "Can you tell what's going on, yet?"

"Yes," he said. "You're being sued for two million dollars for unpaid child support. Mainly for the interest."

"Child support?" Brian asked.

Richard scanned the document. "They had a boy named Heath. He's the other plaintiff in the case."

Karen's stomach knotted up. How could anyone sue her for unpaid child support? "I remember Ernest tried to see the boy, even went to court about it a few times, but Cloris blocked him every time until he gave up. He was pretty sick by then, and getting weaker by the day."

Richard folded the legal papers and put them back into the envelope. "Let me take this and look it over carefully. I need to read up on the law pertaining to child support for a young man Heath's age. We can make an appointment for when you get back from your honeymoon."

They all stood. Brian placed an arm around Karen. "Thank you, Richard. We'll call and pick a date."

Brian walked over to Linda. "Sorry we kept him so late."

Linda smiled as she stood and hugged Brian. "No problem. When work calls, it's best to take care of it right away."

When they were alone, Brian took Karen into his arms and held her close. "First thing tomorrow," he said, "I think you should call Richard and make an appointment with him. I'll get on the phone and postpone the trip to Germany until you've met with him and you're comfortable about leaving town. We won't enjoy our honeymoon unless you do."

How did he know what she was thinking? She pushed away to look into his eyes, loving him more for understanding and saying what she needed to hear. "Are you sure?"

He hugged her again. "I'm positive. We can put everything on hold and reschedule when you're ready." He looked around the cabin. "It looks like we're all done here."

Karen shivered. She should've brought a sweater or coat to wrap around her bare arms, but who thought about warmer clothing in July? The temperature outside was in the nineties, even now with the sun down. Brian liked to set the thermostat low when there was a crowd here. Now that they were the only two left in the room, she was freezing.

She was glad for the help cleaning up, even if they didn't leave town tomorrow as planned. Brian came up behind her and put his arms around her, kissing her tenderly on the back of her neck.

"Well, are you?" he asked.

"What?"

"Ready to go to the house?"

"Oh. Yes. Just making a last minute check of the kitchen. Would you set the thermostat for the night?"

"Sure," he said, but he didn't leave. "Will you be happy living here with me?"

Karen turned and gazed into his eyes. "Yes, of course. I told you I would be. Why do you ask?"

"I don't know. I told the pastor about building this place and all and I began to worry about whether you liked it here as much as I do."

"Well, I may not have the same sentimental reasons for living here you have, but I like it. I'm happy here. I wouldn't hesitate to tell you if I wanted to live somewhere else."

"What do you mean, you don't have the same sentimental attachment? Don't you remember, this is the place where we first made love?"

"Yes, I know. That wasn't my best decision. Or yours, for that matter."

"I'm sorry, I hadn't considered it could be a bad memory for you. Just like the bookmobile, my memories about it were all good and yours were the opposite."

"Don't go apologizing again. I'm not upset by the bookmobile anymore, or this place. It's just that I have different recollections about both of them than you do. Besides, this is totally different than it was thirty years ago. It's built on the same piece of land. That's all."

Brian smiled. "Yeah. But…"

"But nothing." Karen gave him a brilliant smile and looked around. There was nothing else that had to be done. She was thankful for the cleaning help. Still, she lingered in the room, confused about why she didn't want to leave and run to the house to be alone with her new husband.

He fiddled with the thermostat. "So, are we okay here?"

Brian must be anxious to head down the hill to the bedroom. And she was, too. She wasn't stalling. Ever since they had agreed not to be intimate until after the wedding, she'd looked forward to this day. Brian was attentive, as usual, but all she could think about was the lawsuit. She made an effort to smile so as not to alarm him.

"What are you smiling about?" he asked.

"You. I saw how fast you worked to close up the cabin. Why was that?"

"I always work fast."

"Sure. I know what's on your mind, Mr. Donelson."

"You think so? Okay," Brian said, smiling. "I think we're done here." He took her hand as if to lead her out and to the house.

"Did you reset the thermostat?" she asked.

"Yes. All done."

They went outside, locked the door, and walked hand in hand down the lighted rock walk way that led to the main house on the creek. It was a stunning July night with bright stars filling the sky. Karen had grown up on a farm in Iowa and, after moving to Austin, had missed looking at the sky and praising God's beauty. Here, near the lake, the stars were more visible than in town, more like those she saw as a child.

"One of the reasons I like living here," she said as if they had just discussed it, "is the way we can see the stars."

"I love that, too," Brian said.

"Let's sit on the deck and enjoy it some more. Okay?"

She sensed the beginning of a frown on his face that quickly disappeared. "Sure."

"Good. You sit. I'll make us some tea. But first, I want to change into something more comfortable." He was in his tuxedo, but he'd tossed his coat and tie on a chair when they got to the house and the cuff links she'd given him as a wedding gift were hanging in one side of each cuff. He appeared to be relaxed.

She went into the kitchen and turned on the burner under the tea pot before pulling out two cups and saucers. He probably thought she was delaying, but she wasn't. She needed time to unwind before going to bed.

When the pot whistled, she poured the steaming water over the tea bags. Brian carried the tea tray outside and placed it on the table where he often had breakfast. They sipped tea and watched the sky without speaking.

Brian broke the silence first, keeping his eyes to the heavens. "I hope you won't take this as a criticism or a suggestion that I want you to be different. I learned a long time ago that feelings just are and not something we should try to control. I'm not suggesting you change how you feel about your past. I'm just curious why the reminder of Ernest hit you so hard."

Karen had wondered that herself. She didn't have an answer. To make things worse, she had to hide her feelings from him tonight, maybe until she got past it and she hated starting out their marriage that way. She continued to study the stars and sipping her tea, not knowing what to say.

"Now I've hurt you," Brian said. "I'm sorry."

Karen set the tea cup and saucer on the side table between them and turned toward Brian. "No. You didn't. It's a fair question and I understand why you asked it."

"I asked it knowing you're a strong person with a closeness to God I wish I had. And you've dealt with tougher problems during your life."

"You're right. I've had to be tough," she said. "To be honest, I've asked myself the same question since the wedding. I don't understand why I feel the way I do."

Brian sipped his tea then placed his cup and saucer next to hers. "Knowing you the way I do, I'm surprised you're letting this bother you. Just look at all we went through in the past year. Each revelation eased the weight of the problem when we shared it, rather than making it worse by trying to deal with it on our own."

"I remember the times when neither one of us believed we'd ever be happy, much less married to each other."

Brian continued. "You kept the miscarriage a secret from everyone, thinking you had caused it by the anger you felt toward me. You went through it alone, without family and without friends. And without me. That was my fault, not yours."

"It was a sad and lonely time in my life. Only later, I prayed about it and made it manageable. I must admit now it wasn't until I told you about it that I was released from the guilt. At the time I thought telling you would be the end of any chance for us to reconcile, especially since you had just learned your daughter wasn't yours and she was the reason you left me in the first place."

She reached out to touch his arm. "I had to tell you about the miscarriage. I want everything to be open between us. I thank God for the way you accepted my confession and wanted to take all the blame for my having to face the pregnancy alone."

"See, that's what I'm talking about," he said. He sounded strong, but she saw his eyes were glistening. "Look at all the problems we faced in the past thirty years. Both of us. Now this. Why can't we work together and dispel one more problem?"

Karen heard the muted sound of a boat passing in the distance. She took her husband into her arms and held him close. The warmth of his body against hers excited her. If only she'd married Brian when they first fell in love, before Ernest, and Steve. But then they wouldn't have their wonderful daughters. *Oh, God, why? Why have you put me in the midst of this turmoil?*

An owl hooted, adding its music to the water smacking against the shore. "I can't talk about this anymore. But thanks for being so supportive and understanding. It's not the best discussion to have on one's wedding night."

"I love you. I'll listen anytime. Are you ready for bed?"

"Yes."

She'd thought she was, but it turned out she wasn't.

***

Karen woke with a jolt as the sun began its daily ritual. It took a minute to remember where she was. Brian slept peacefully next to her, his presence reminding her how she'd suggested they wait until morning to make love for the first time in more than thirty years. Now was the time. Even though she wanted to, she was reluctant to wake him. There was no doubt she loved him dearly. Still, she slid out of bed as quietly as possible and walked toward the bathroom. She stopped halfway there and looked back to see if he was sleeping. He was. She smiled at the sight he made. His tousled hair reminded her of the longer, curlier hair he'd had in college. She continued on to the bathroom and shut the door behind her.

The large glass block window let light in without allowing anyone to see in or out. As the sun lit up the room, she saw a shadow too tall to be an animal pass near the window. Who could that be? There were no neighbors nearby. She went to the family room. Its large plate glass window offered a view of the same side of the house as the bathroom. She ducked behind the drapes and peeped out. Could she see anyone? She should wake Brian and ask him who it could be. Perhaps a deer? She stood by the window watching, hardly breathing, waiting for the shadowy object to appear. When it did, she jumped back and gasped. A man. She couldn't see his face as he ran from the house and disappeared behind the trees that surrounded the property.

"You okay?" Brian asked, standing in the door to the hallway.

CHAPTER FOUR

Brian scratched his head and rubbed his eyes trying to figure out what was going on. When he woke up alone, he went to find Karen. He'd found her hiding behind the drapes in the family room.

"I don't know," she said as she walked to him. "Just after sunrise I saw something weird through the bathroom window, so I came in here to get a better look."

A sudden surge of adrenalin filled Brian's wakening body. There shouldn't be anyone close to the house. Why hadn't she called him sooner?

"Was it a man?" Brian had told Liz the library could use the bookmobile while they were away on their honeymoon, and she'd said someone would be by to pick it up, but they wouldn't do it at the crack of dawn on a Sunday.

"I think so. But he was just a blur as he moved past here and disappeared into the trees."

The idea of a trespasser being so close to the house was not a positive one. "It was probably just someone going to the creek. Someone who didn't know this was private property."

"Do you think so?"

"Could be. I'll go look around if you want."

"No. Not now." She pointed toward the wooded area off to the left. "He moved through those trees at a fast pace. He's probably long gone."

"You know," Brian said, remembering. "I didn't lock the gate last night. It was late by the time Richard left and I forgot all about it. Maybe someone drove in then realized they were at a private home."

"That's possible. Do you want to go back to bed?" she asked.

Did she mean him or them? Brian wasn't positive. Last night she'd said they should wait until morning when they were rested. Is that what she meant? With all the distractions they should probably wait until they get to Germany, but he didn't want her to think he wasn't interested. He wasn't comfortable talking about it and, besides, he could be misreading her.

He looked toward the bedroom with a longing in his heart, and then turned toward the office. "I'm wide awake now. I better make those phone calls about our honeymoon. Do you mind starting the coffee?"

He called the airlines and hotels and cancelled their reservations. Afterwards he went to the kitchen where he poured a cup of coffee and went out to join Karen on the dock. He was in his pajamas, but there were no neighbors to see him and few boats passed by this narrow part of the creek leading to Lake Austin, especially early on Sunday mornings.

This was the best time of day to be outside in July in central Texas. When the sun rose higher, it would be too hot and sticky and it'd stay that way until dark. He usually had breakfast on the dock and was glad Karen had moved naturally toward his favorite place without their talking about it. He sat next to her so they could both look at the water. He sipped his coffee.

"Did you talk to Richard?" he asked.

"Yes. He's going to meet us at the office this afternoon at two."

"Great. I'm glad he's willing to do it today."

"Me too." She lifted the cup to her mouth, pausing as she did. "He probably wants to help us get on to our honeymoon."

They sat in silence. A bird sang a morning tune. A boat motor hummed away in the distance, probably on the main part of the lake. Brian had purchased fishing equipment and gotten his license after moving there, but he'd yet to catch anything. Perhaps he should get a boat so that he could go to deeper parts of the lake.

"Any problems cancelling the reservations?" she asked.

"No. I told them I'd call back as soon as we have firm dates. We're not cancelling our honeymoon. Just postponing it."

"I'm sorry to cause this trouble."

"You didn't cause anything. I've thought about this case all morning. I think this was part of their plan. They wanted to mess up our trip."

"What?" She looked at him with eyes wide opened. "How'd you come up with that?"

"Look at the lawsuit. Who is the defendant? Karen Williams Donelson. Not Karen Williams, but Karen Donelson. This Heath character, or more likely his mother, knew you were getting married and knew when. The legal paperwork had to have been done before the wedding."

Karen's usual smile turned into a frown. "You're right. And you know what else? I think some of them came to the wedding."

"What?" Brian asked.

"Remember the photographer I asked you about? I don't know who he was. The one I hired was clearly irritated with him getting in the way so I know he didn't work for her. And he disappeared as soon as the wedding was over. We'll never see those photos, I'm sure. I also saw another guy there who was frowning while everyone else was happy for us."

"You sure that wasn't an old boyfriend?" Brian smiled to let her know he was joking.

Karen looked serious. "Why would they serve the papers at our wedding right before we were to leave on our honeymoon? The only reason would be to cause us to cancel the trip, or at least take some of the enjoyment out of it. Maybe we should have waited to react to the papers until after the honeymoon. Perhaps we're doing what they wanted us to do and then they'll drop the lawsuit."

"No. I think there's more to it." He paused, unsure how to word what he wanted to say. "I don't want to belittle the successful career you've had as a teacher. With the pension you earned and the income from the farm you inherited from your parents, you could live comfortably for the rest of your life."

"But—"

"But, I think they waited until you married me, knowing I have enough money to pay the two million they're asking for."

"I considered that," she said. "I'm doing okay, but I don't have anything they could take."

"So," he asked, "the question is, what do we do now?"

"What do you mean? I thought we agreed to let Richard handle it."

"Well, yes, but we need to talk about what we want him to do. I think we should tell him to settle as quickly as possible for as little as possible. I bet he can get them down to a couple hundred thousand or less."

"Are you kidding?" Karen stared at him with piercing eyes. "You want to pay them off? That'd be admitting I'm guilty. And I'm not. I didn't do what they claim."

"Sometimes it's not a question of guilt or innocence. Often, the best way to handle a frivolous lawsuit is to settle and get it over with. Cut your losses and get them out of your life. Or, as Liz used to ask me, 'Would you rather be happy or right?'"

Karen stood and walked to end of the dock with her back to Brian. "Well, I'll never settle."

Brian went to her and put his arm around her. She didn't move away, but a strange coldness greeted him. "I'm sorry. I assumed we were discussing what to do. I gave my suggestion, now you give yours.

She turned toward him and locked her eyes on his. "I want to know why they filed the lawsuit." Her voice filled the dock and spilled out over the water. Not loud, but full and stern. "Nothing happens without a reason. God wants me to do something. I don't know what or why, but I'm sure it's not to throw money at the problem. If I use your money to pay them off, I'll never know why I've been called to face this situation."

"*Our* money," he said, and paused a few seconds. "I'm sorry. I understand what you're saying. It's still not natural for me to include God in everything that happens in life. I love that you can and I'm learning how. We'll do it your way. I'm sorry I brought it up."

She smiled. "Thanks for understanding. I'm just sorry you have to go through this with me. Especially now, so soon after our marriage."

He took her into his arms and held her silently.

She pulled him closer. "I love you," she said.

***

Later that afternoon they went to Richard's office on Congress Avenue. Karen couldn't resist bussing Brian on the cheek as she walked through the door he held open for her. He'd handled her little tantrum better than she could have expected. He hadn't been a wimp about it, either. He'd voiced his opinion and she hers. But she had to give him credit for knowing not to go on their honeymoon before she talked to her attorney.

Love wasn't enough sometimes. They had a lot to learn about each other, like how to have an argument or fight and come out clean. They'd both been single long enough to need a refresher course in how to have a successful marriage. Neither of them had been happily married before, but that didn't mean they couldn't be this time.

Richard met them in the lobby before they had a chance to sit. He wore gray slacks with a dark blue knit shirt that had a gold golf course emblem on it. "Come in, Karen." He motioned toward an open door.

"Good afternoon, Richard," Karen said, walking toward to door. "Thanks for seeing us today."

Brian turned to a group of chairs in the waiting area, and grabbed a magazine on the side table. Karen stopped and faced him. "Brian, will you come with me?"

She knew he was offering her privacy, but she wanted him to join her. "I'd like you to be an extra set of ears to help me remember and understand what's going on here. Okay?"

"Yes, of course." He tossed the magazine and followed her into Richard's office.

After they were seated, Richard pulled out the legal papers and placed them on the desk. "I want to know more about the circumstances of your marriage to Ernest."

"When we married, I didn't think of Ernest as my husband. Cathy called it a marriage of convenience yesterday. That's a pretty good description of it." She crossed her legs and took a deep breath.

"Since I married him to provide insurance, it may have been illegal. I don't know. I was idealistic and didn't care. Looking back now, I realize it wasn't the best thing to do."

"Were you coerced by anyone in any way?" Richard asked.

"No, not at all. Cloris had divorced him as soon as she learned his days were numbered. They hadn't been married long, a matter of months, I think, and she'd insisted on a prenuptial since he'd lost everything in a previous divorce and was too sick to work regularly. She married him to give the baby a name and then wouldn't let Ernest see his infant son after the divorce."

"So, you married him to take care of him?" Richard asked.

Karen turned toward Brian. He smiled encouragingly. "Yes. That's part of it. No one should have to die alone or with strangers. By getting married, he became eligible for my insurance plan. It allowed him better quality of care. But, mainly, I wanted him to have someone with him who cared for him."

Richard nodded. "I see."

Talking about Ernest and the time leading up to his death pained her more than she wanted to admit. It appeared she didn't have a choice. According to the laws of the state of Texas, she had to respond to the lawsuit and that meant she had to recall that time with Ernest and the way his body gradually shut down. And, according to the laws of God, her response to the lawsuit had to be more than a cash settlement. Perhaps that wasn't a law, but it was a strong feeling she had and she'd learned long ago to trust her instincts.

Richard sat with both arms on his desk, focused on Karen as if waiting for her to continue.

"What I don't understand," she said, "is why I'm responsible for Ernest's child support payments. Can't you just call them and tell them how ridiculous that is?"

Richard laughed. "I wish it were that simple. Based on my initial reading, they think they have a case. So, we have to answer them through the court. It appears they intend to prove you took all of your former husband's assets, leaving nothing for his child."

"He didn't have any assets." Karen tried not to say it loudly, but she wanted to scream. "That's the reason I married him."

"I understand." Richard held the document up and waved it. "I'm just telling you what they're contending in here. It'll be our job to disprove the allegations. That shouldn't be too difficult."

"Well, that's good to hear," Karen said. "But it all happened more than twenty years ago. What if I don't have proof of anything that far back?" Unwanted tears gathered in her eyes. *Stop it!*

Brian placed a hand on her shoulder as he addressed Richard. "Isn't there a statute of limitation?" he asked.

Richard turned to Brian. "I did some research on that this morning. In Texas, and probably many states, the statute of limitations for collecting child support favors the child. In Texas all claims must be filed before the child's twenty-second birthday. In this case the child turned twenty-two one week after the case was filed. They filed just in time."

Richard placed the papers on his desk and clasped his hands on top of the document. "Look, I can see this is upsetting you. Here's what I'll do. I'll talk to the attorney representing the plaintiff and find out more about this. Nothing needs to be done by you until after your honeymoon. If I learn of anything that's time-sensitive, I'll call you immediately. Otherwise, I suggest you go enjoy your honeymoon."

"Are you sure?" She wanted to pass the burden to Richard, but it was hard to let go. "I'd hate to be out of the country and unable to defend myself."

Richard smiled. "Don't worry. These cases tend to move slowly. Besides, I can represent you if anything urgent comes up. All we need to do today is have you sign a paper saying I'm your attorney and I'll file it with the court and send a copy to the plaintiff's attorney. Then they have to notify me about the case instead of you."

Karen glanced at Brian and then faced Richard. "You understand, I don't want to settle. Unless they drop the case, I want to proceed with my defense. I'm innocent and I don't want one cent going to these people."

Richard narrowed his eyes. "I understand what you're saying. As your attorney, I may occasionally discuss options with you. You may decide later it's in your best interest to change your mind. No matter what you decide, I represent you and what you want to do. Now, let me take care of it and you two go enjoy your honeymoon."

Karen smiled at Brian. "Can you get us on the next flight to Germany?"

CHAPTER FIVE

The next day, Karen gazed out the window of the train as they traveled from Hanover to Hildesheim. It wasn't one of those super-fast trains Brian had told her about. On this one she had time to soak in the old-world countryside as they journeyed. She saw trees scattered between acres of cultivated fields with a variety of vegetation in full bloom, none of which she could name. They passed through several small towns and villages giving her an up close view of the homes and stores along the tracks.

Karen's stomach growled. "Do they have food on this train?"

"I'm sure they do," Brian said, "but we're getting close to Hildesheim. We can eat there."

"Oh, I didn't realize it was such a short trip. I meant to look at a map before we left home, but I didn't find time. You're going to have to be my guide, okay?" She leaned into him and patted his leg.

He smiled. "I'm no expert, though. Amy and I were here when she was in high school, probably twelve years ago. What I remember most is the happiness I experienced for the first time in years. But it might have been due to spending more time alone with Amy rather than being in Germany."

"I wondered about that when you first told me the story of your trip here," Karen said. "It doesn't matter if it was Hildesheim or the situation. I wanted to visit the place that makes you smile when you talk about it."

Brian glanced out the window as the train decelerated. "We're here."

They gathered their bags and stepped onto a covered platform, went down the stairs and through a tunnel to the Bahnhof, the train station proper. They had all their belongings in two carry-ons. It meant washing clothes along the way, but Brian had said smaller suitcases made traveling more enjoyable. As they went up the second set of stairs she was glad she'd agreed.

"Okay," Brian said as they walked out of the station. "It looks about the same as I remember from my last trip here."

She grinned, eager to move around and explore after the long trip. "What do we do now? Should we get one of those taxis?"

"Taxi?" he said. "No. They're for tourists who brought too many suitcases. Our hotel is just up there." He pointed toward the street in front of the station. "Besides, we've been sitting all day. I know I could use the exercise. Follow me."

He led her to a pedestrian subway under a busy street and kept walking onto what could once have been a street but was now for pedestrians and delivery trucks only.

Karen's hunger gnawed at her again, but she was too fascinated by the stores and the people to complain. Not only was this her first trip to Germany, this was her first trip to Europe. She tried to read some of the signs in the shop windows, though she couldn't understand most of them.

Brian stopped soon after they got to the pedestrian way. "I promised you we'd eat when we got here. Do you want to watch for a place along here, or wait until we check in so we can leave our bags?"

"I'm famished. If you see something you like, stop."

"Okay." Brian veered to the right and stopped in front of a bakery. "This place may have sandwiches. Or we could snack on a pastry and eat a meal later."

"Mmm. Looks good. Have you eaten here before?"

"Probably, but I don't remember for sure. I remember the smell, though. There's nothing more inviting than the aroma of baked bread and pastries right out of the oven."

"I like your idea of a snack here and meal later." Karen pulled her carryon to the display cabinet and admired the tarts, croissants, and a variety of other delights she didn't recognize. Freshly baked loaves of bread poked out of a nearby rack.

Karen selected a custard tart covered with glazed strawberries and Brian asked for a pastry that looked like an American bear claw. They ordered two coffees as well. An Americano for him and a regular espresso for her. They found a table outside in front of the bakery and ate while watching people walk by. Since the pedestrian way was near the train station, they weren't the only ones with suitcases. Young men and women in dark suits pulled carry-ons past them, most of them moving rapidly as if they were on a schedule.

A family of four struggled along with eight large suitcases. The woman attempted to pull two bags on wheels, but the luggage wanted to go in different directions.

Another man came into view. "Look at that guy," Karen said, nodding toward a tall, chunky-looking fellow in a white tee shirt that didn't cover his belly. His faded jeans were cinched in tightly with a cowboy belt. On his head, slightly askew, was an English driving cap that didn't match the rest of his clothing.

Brian scanned the area.

"Hey," Karen said. "He just took our picture. Did you see that?"

The young man walked away, the camera hung loosely in his right hand, its long lens clearly evident.

"That guy in the funny-looking hat? I see the camera. Are you sure he took a photo of us?"

"I'm positive. Strange, huh? I may be paranoid, but the first thing I thought of was the lawsuit. Do you think he's following us?"

"I doubt it. We just finalized our reservations yesterday. He probably wanted a picture of an attractive woman."

She shook her head, smiling a little at his nonsense. "There's something unusual about that guy. If it wasn't so hard to believe, I'd say he looked like that mystery photographer at the wedding."

"Really?"

"He's dressed different, but he looks American."

"I think he was wearing a cowboy belt, but you can get those here as well as back home."

"I guess." Karen licked her empty fork. "That was delicious."

Brian nodded. "Ready to go? We're not far from the hotel. Let's register and find a place for a real meal. Last time I was here there was an excellent restaurant near our hotel. Amy's choir friends and their parents all loved it. I did, too."

"I'm ready." They put their plates and cups on the counter and grabbed their luggage to continue the trek toward the hotel.

Muffled street noise turned into a cacophony as they turned the corner on the way to the hotel.

"Must be market day," Brian said. "Let's see what they have."

The town square was covered with booths, each surrounded by shoppers. Sellers were describing the excellence of their merchandise and buyers were asking for better deals. Everyone talked at once, and Karen didn't understand a word they said. Even so, she loved the guttural sounds, the expressive ways of speaking and the rhythm of the language. She turned toward a smell that caught the attention of her nose and made her mouth water. She looked back to make sure Brian saw her. She didn't want to get separated in the crowd. He smiled at her and nodded for her to go ahead.

She got to a table stacked high with bread. All types of bread. All sizes and shapes, so fresh she could smell the yeasty aroma. Customers stuffed unwrapped loaves into canvas shopping bags. Next to the bread was the meat section. There were meats she'd never seen before. Some raw and some smoked. The next table displayed a selection of fruits and vegetables. She picked up a large white root vegetable to examine it, wondering what it was.

"*Nicht berühren!*" the woman behind the table scolded.

Karen turned to Brian.

"She said, 'don't touch.'"

Karen hastily set it down. "What is this thing?"

Brian shook his head and turned toward the woman who was straightening the display. "*Was ist das?*"

The woman answered in German.

"What's that in English?" he asked.

She shrugged.

When they got to the end of the first row of booths, Brian stopped and pointed ahead to a building six floors high with an open-air restaurant on the street level. "That's where we're staying."

Everything about the hotel seemed small to Karen, including the elevator. There was barely room for the two of them with their carry-ons. When the elevator door closed, Brian moved to her and kissed her. She melted into his arms and the kiss continued until they reached their floor.

He unlocked the door to their room and motioned her in. It was small, but she loved it as soon as she looked around. A large open window overlooked the square and the market activity they had visited. No glass panes, no screens, just open. Behind the curtains she found windows folded to the sides waiting to be put into service during the winter months. The standard-sized bed took up most of the floor space. Sleeping together would be a challenge for people used to more spacious beds. Oh, well, it was their honeymoon. She wished she wasn't so tired or jet-lagged or whatever it was.

Next, she checked the bathroom. In the corner of the miniature room was a tiny shower, not much larger than one she'd once seen on a boat. No bathtub. The toilet was between the shower and a petite sink.

They'd planned to leave right away, but they both took time to wash up. Still, it wasn't long before they were on the street, looking for the restaurant where Brian had eaten with Amy and her high school choir. They turned left on what appeared to be a main thoroughfare. Unleashed dogs walked alongside their masters without barking or growling. The animals stayed with their owners, even when they went into stores and banks.

Brian and Karen passed an old man sitting on a bench. He didn't appear to be a derelict like in some larger cities around the world. He had a full gray beard with a pipe poking out from where his mouth would be. His cheeks were red. A green corduroy hat sat back far enough to show the beginning of his balding head. He followed her with his eyes, taking her in as she studied him. Karen was focused on the man when he suddenly locked his eyes with hers. Just before walking past, she nodded and he nodded back. What caught Karen's attention was his age. He could have lived during World War II, perhaps he'd been a soldier in Hitler's army? Had he killed Americans? Had his home been bombed? Had any of his family been killed?

After they were well past the old man, Karen took Brian's hand. "You told me most of Hildesheim was leveled by allied bombers during the final days of World War II, but the buildings all look old to me. Is that possible?"

"I asked the same question when I was here before. Our guide said all the buildings were reconstructed from photos taken before the war. They used the same stones for the exterior when possible. The insides are more modern."

Karen wondered what it must have been like to live in a place where war was a daily lesson in survival for so long. She wondered if the Germans born after 1945 understood what their parents endured.

"It's here," Brian said. The restaurant he'd remembered was inside a triangular-shaped lot where two streets crossed at an angle. They took an outdoor table under the tall trees. Small gray birds flitted around on the ground scavenging for crumbs between the tables. Brian ordered schnitzel and dumplings and Karen selected bratwurst with coleslaw and hot potato salad. As soon as the food was served, they stopped talking.

Afterwards, Brian paid the bill and led Karen in a direction away from the way they came. "Let me show you the church where Amy sang. I believe it's just up this street here."

They walked hand in hand. When they got to a huge church, Karen stopped. "Is this it?"

"Not this one. This is St. Andrew's," Brian said, looking at the map the hotel desk clerk gave him. "According to this information, construction began in 1389. It was destroyed in 1945 in an air raid and reconstruction began in 1956. It was rededicated in 1965." He pointed to the top of the church. "Amy and I went up there. The view of the city is breathtaking. We can do that tomorrow, if you want to."

"I'd like that."

They continued to walk.

"Ah, here it is," he said. "St. Lamberti's Church."

"What does the brochure say about it?"

Brian studied the map. "Not much. All it says is that 'construction on this Gothic parish church in the new section of the city began in 1474.'"

"There's so much more history here than in the States."

They went into the church. Karen turned in a circle, taking in the beauty of the place. "It's striking," she said.

"Yes. And you should hear music performed here. The old churches were built before microphones and speakers. Amy's choir sang without amplification and you could hear every word from anywhere in the church. The sound was deeper and more stunning than usual."

They walked to the altar and examined the pulpit. It appeared to be as old as the church. Seated on the first row Karen and Brian silently soaked in the splendor. They got up together without planning it and walked out, hand in hand.

When they were outside, Brian stopped and looked into her eyes. "While we were sitting there, I remembered another place I'd like to show you. Come."

He led her further away from the hotel, through a garden, or park. Karen preferred a nap, but she didn't want to disappoint Brian. He seemed excited about being back to the place where he'd once been so happy.

They walked past another enormous, ancient church, onto a residential street lined with trees. At the end of the street was a small park with a cubic-shaped structure in the center.

Brian pulled out the travel guide. "This is a monument to the Jews who were driven out of town or killed. On the map it's referred to as the Monument on the Lappenberg. This, it says, is where Hildesheim's synagogue once stood, consecrated in 1849 and burned to the ground in 1938."

Karen walked around the monument. "What is all the writing on it?" she asked.

"We'd need someone to translate it, but I remember the main theme is to remember what happened so it won't happen again."

They took a leisurely route back to the hotel and Brian showed her more sights along the way. It was early in the evening by the time they returned, tired and ready for dinner. They had a small meal of meat and cheese with some exceptionally good bread at the small restaurant on the market square below their room.

In their room, Karen showered first. When she came out she saw Brian had found an English-speaking news station on the TV. All was well with the world, he told her.

While he took his shower, she curled up in bed to watch the news.

That was the last thing she remembered until the sound of someone retching woke her. She sat up in the dark room, suddenly alert, wondering if Brian was okay. She quickly found he was sleeping peacefully next to her. She listened again and decided the sound had come from outside. She went to the window and looked around. The noise was coming from a person near a tree, not far from where they had eaten the meat and cheese earlier. The poor man was hunched over throwing up. Other than the puking sound and some laughter from his pals, the area was quiet. The tables and tents were gone.

As she stared out the window, she saw a flash and wondered if it was lightning. It looked more like the flash of a camera, but why would anyone be taking pictures in the dark? She picked up her watch and could barely make out the time by holding it near the window. It was a quarter past three. She must have fallen asleep while Brian was showering. Poor man. Would he ever have his wedding night? *Would I?*

She was wide awake now. She went back to the bedroom and started to wake him. He was sleeping so deeply, she decided not to. There was plenty of time for a real honeymoon.

***

Brian sat up in bed, dazed, unsure why he was sitting. Was it a dream? Was there an intruder? He scanned the room. Where was Karen? He heard a sound he recognized. His cell phone vibrated on the lamp table next to the bed. He remembered turning the ringer off before going to bed, but the constant thump, thump, thump must be what awakened him. He grabbed the phone as he jumped out of bed. He had to find Karen. Why was she calling?

He was dizzy. "Hello. Karen?"

That was wrong. She was somewhere close by; she wouldn't be calling him on his cell.

"Karen? You mean she's not there? Don't tell me you two have split up?" Ron laughed. His friend's usual laugh, too loud and too long, brought Brian back to reality.

"Ron? Hold on a minute." Brian was awake now. He tossed the phone on the bed and searched for Karen in earnest. The bathroom door was closed and the shower running. There was dim light coming in through the window, making long shadows across the room. He retraced his steps to the bed, picked up his phone to check the time. It was five in the morning.

He held the phone to his ear. "Do you know what time it is here? What's so important you had to call this early?"

"Sorry," Ron said without sounding like he understood what the word meant. "I waited as long as I could. This is important."

"I hope so." Brian felt off kilter. Something about Karen, but he wasn't sure why. He paced the few steps between the bed and bathroom.

"You know the supply contract with that Brussels brush company?"

"Yeah." Brian stopped and put his ear to the bathroom door.

"The previous owners didn't renew when it came due. It's expired."

"Are you sure? That contract gave us exclusive rights in North and South America. We've got to get that agreement extended."

"I know. That's why I'm calling. And I don't know what else got goofed up before we regained control of the company."

Brian was the majority stock holder and CEO after getting control of the company back from the group that nearly bankrupted it. Ron was his chief financial officer and he managed the Redondo Beach, California company from his office in Austin.

Brian heard the sound of water splashing in the bathroom so he backed away, toward the window. "Have they signed with another company yet?" he asked.

"No," Ron said. "They called to say they plan to go out for bids tomorrow. When I explained the situation and told them you are back in charge of the company, they agreed to extend the contract, but only if they can meet with you right away."

"Why can't you take care of it from there?"

"After the problems they had with the previous owners, they want to see you in person. I don't need to tell you how important this contract is."

Ron could be crude at times, but when it came to business, he didn't joke around. He was right to call. This contract was important to the future of the company. "Did you tell them I'm on my honeymoon?"

"Hey, they were thrilled to know you were in Europe. Karen will understand. Where is she, by the way?" He laughed again.

"That's not funny. She's in the shower if you must know. The call woke me and I must have been dreaming. Now drop it."

"Drop what?" Karen asked, standing outside the bathroom door, and dressed only in a towel.

The towel was extremely distracting. He smiled and held up a hand toward Karen. "What did you say, Ron?"

"You're booked into a wonderful place in Bruges. You can have the rest of your honeymoon there. Your train leaves in one hour. Can you make it?"

"I guess. Okay. It sounds like we don't have a choice." He turned toward Karen wondering how to tell her they had to leave. He said good bye to Ron and threw the phone on the bed. When he looked up, Karen was gone and the bathroom door closed. He sat on the bed with his head in his hands. Nothing had gone the way he'd hoped. When he'd finished his shower last night and gotten into bed, Karen slept soundly so he decided not to wake her. To be honest, he was a little tired himself. Not *too* tired, but he thought how much better it would be when they were both rested and emotionally ready.

While Karen had slept last night, Brian had stood at the window looking out over the square. An enticing spicy aroma of sausage and kraut wafted up from the street. A quarter moon peeked over the building on the right, encasing it in a blue wash that filled their room. She appeared to be calm and relaxed as she slept. All the tension he'd seen on her face since she'd been sued was gone. He bowed his head and thanked God.

"Dear, Lord," he'd said aloud, but softly, "give me the ability and knowledge to help Karen. You know she's going through a rough time and you know how much I love her. But I don't know what to say or what to do. Give me a sign. Let me know when I'm on the right track. I love her so much and I want her to have the happiness she deserves. Amen."

He'd watched her sleep a while longer before he finally fell asleep himself.

He was lost in his thoughts when Karen came out of the bathroom fully dressed.

"Brian? Are you okay?"

He stood. "Yes. I'm fine." He took her in his arms and hugged her. "A problem came up with the company. An important situation, but one I can solve. However, it means leaving here and going to Bruges."

"Where's Bruges?"

"It's a wonderful place in Belgium. You'll like it."

"When do we go?" she said, smiling.

Her smile reminded him of how happy she looked as she slept last night.

CHAPTER SIX

The six-hour trip from Hildesheim was more fun than Karen thought it would be when Brian described it to her. She saw places she'd heard of before, but had never thought she'd visit. The first part of the trip took them to Frankfurt where they changed to a train to Brussels. A third train took them the rest of the way. The cars were comfortable, and the food was tasty and interesting. She also liked zooming past ancient wooden homes in the smaller towns and villages and seeing the green fields between the cities.

"I don't know why Ron booked us a rental car in Bruges," Brian said, looking at the itinerary the desk clerk in Hildesheim had printed for them. "Once we get to the room where we're staying, we won't need a car. Every place we want to go is within walking distance. Besides, it's difficult to maneuver a modern vehicle in towns built for a horse and buggy."

Karen took the paperwork from Brian. "It looks like it's prepaid. Let's use it to get to the room. That'll save the cost of a cab. We can turn it in tomorrow."

Karen was ready to get to the room. She wanted to be alone with her man and hold him close in a way she couldn't last night. She was rested now; the jetlag no longer a concern. There was something else about today. Something she couldn't put her finger on. For some reason she liked Bruges better than Hildesheim. She grabbed his arm and pulled him close. The surprised look on his face that quickly turned into a smile pleased her.

They signed the paperwork at the car rental agency, got the keys and instructions on how to get to the bed and breakfast Ron had booked. The agent drew a route on the map with a wide yellow highlighter to show the way. The place where they were going was inside an area surrounded by water and the route took many turns and twists. The agent explained the circuitous route was due to one-way streets. "It isn't difficult."

They found the first bridge, but the streets highlighted in yellow on the map didn't match the names of the streets they were on. They had either taken a wrong turn somewhere or the agent didn't know what he was talking about. One-way streets popped up unexpectedly. Cars were parked on curbs, some even apparently abandoned in the middle of the road, which made most streets one lane with the two-way traffic taking turns to get through the tight places.

Karen tried to watch the map as Brian drove but soon gave up. Nothing on the map matched the world in front of them and there was no way to turn around and go back to try again.

"Stop here," Karen said, pointing to a car pulling out of what looked like half a parking spot. "I'll go in that hotel and see if they can help us."

Karen opened the door, but before she got out, a man walked up to the car. "Can I help?" he said, pointing to the map she held.

"Yes, please. We're looking for this place." She handed him the bed and breakfast confirmation.

He pulled out his cell phone and made a call. Karen couldn't understand what he said. He hung up and handed the paper back to her.

"Follow me."

He climbed into a car and waited while Brian moved in behind him. The man drove away slowly while Brian and Karen followed close behind. They went down one street after another, all narrow and crowded. It seemed like they'd gone around in circles for about ten minutes before the car they were following stopped. The driver pointed to a door and drove on. Karen looked up at the building and saw it was the one they were looking for.

"We're here," Karen said to Brian who acted as if he wanted to follow the car but couldn't find it.

She waved toward the helpful man to thank him, but his car was out of sight.

"Are you sure this is the place?" he asked.

"This is it. See the name beside the door, and the number. What a trip that was, and the guy didn't hang around long enough for us to say thanks."

"He probably does it a lot." Brian stared at the map. "I can understand how people get lost here. I still don't know where we are."

Brian looked around. "Okay, we have to park – we can't leave the car here. Why don't you get out so we don't lose sight of the building while I try to figure out where I can park."

A good fifteen minutes later, she watched Brian hustle their luggage along the sidewalk toward her. He must have gone several blocks away, and the fact that he remembered his way back raised her already sky-high admiration of the wonderful guy who'd married her.

His determined expression made her smile. The smile faltered as she saw someone else watching him. Only the man's head and shoulders were visible as he leaned out from behind the building next to the bed and breakfast. She didn't know whether to mention it to Brian or not. Probably just some curious local watching the tourists. Perhaps Brian had taken the man's favorite parking spot.

They grabbed their bags and went into the three-story building. It appeared to have once been a large single-family dwelling. A young woman in a costume of some type came out of one of the rooms and met them in the entryway. Her skirt was patterned in bright shades of reds and blues although her blouse was plain white. It wasn't the type of outfit you'd find a person wearing at home. The beam on her face and the way she carried herself showed she was happy and healthy and enjoyed life—the type of person whose attitude rubs off on everyone around them.

"Welcome. You must be the Donelsons." Her voice was a smile that lit up the room.

"Yes. I'm Karen and this is Brian."

"I'm Tea deJong. Let me show you to your room." She shook hands and turned toward the stairs. "I guess the information office warned you about this place." She ran up the stairs.

Karen looked at Brian with eyebrows arched, then turned her gaze back to Tea. "Warned us?"

Tea grinned, looking at them as if they shared some humorous secret. "You know, about the room."

"Uh, no," Brian said. "I guess not. A business associate back home made the reservation for us. It was a last minute thing. What's wrong with the room?"

"Wrong?" Tea stopped in the middle of stairs and studied them. "There's nothing wrong. I think it's a wonderful room, but some people call it different. Odd, perhaps." She continued to smile. "Don't worry. Most people love it here."

"Oh, well," Karen said. "I'm sure it'll be fine. Long as we have a bed and some privacy. We're on our honeymoon."

Tea winked. "We'll have to see what you think about privacy after you get to the room."

Brian glanced toward Karen with a slight smile and mouthed a "Yikes."

Their room was on the second floor near the top of the stairs. Tea opened the door and motioned for them to enter. "Well, you better take a look and see if you want to stay here or not. It won't hurt my feelings. Not everyone appreciates my idea of art."

Karen entered first and laughed loudly. "I see. We won't be alone here."

Costumed mannequins sat in several places around the room, one on the sofa, another in a chair at the dining table. A third one sat in a chair near a window as if looking out; all dressed like burlesque dancers from the Victorian period with ankle-length layered dresses. While most of their bodies were covered by the dresses and hose, they appeared sensual.

Tea stood at the door waiting for their decision.

Brian turned in a circle while scanning the room. "It's unusual."

Karen peeked in the bathroom. No mannequins there, but the toilet was on a pedestal, not unlike a small throne.

"I like it," she declared. If anyone asked, she wouldn't be able to explain why, but she loved the room. She'd never seen anything like it, but it was exactly where she needed to be.

"Well, if you like it, I do, too," Brian said.

"All right, then," Tea said. "I'll leave you two alone. Breakfast is between six and ten. We don't have a dining room, but we have a table in each room." She pointed to the small table with three chairs, two of which were empty. The mannequin in the third chair leaned its elbows on the table as if waiting to be served. "Just let me know your preferences by ten each night and what time you want your meal served." She started to leave, but turned back. "And call me if you need anything. Bye bye."

Tea might be gone, but her positive attitude hung around, getting all over Karen, and she was happy for it. Brian looked happier, too. The tension she'd seen in his face during the difficult drive to the bed and breakfast disappeared.

"We should have asked her to recommend a place for dinner," Karen said.

Brian nodded. "Yeah. I love to try the places where the locals eat. I've not done that here." He checked his watch. "I've got that meeting coming up. Would you ask Tea where we should eat?"

"Sure. Are you okay with this place?" She motioned around the room. "I feel comfortable here, but I want you to like it, too."

Brian glanced around the room again. "I have to say I've never seen anything like this before, but I have no problems with it. It's fun."

"Good." Karen started unpacking. "The fun could be part Tea. She's a joy to be around."

Brian went into the bathroom and shut the door. Shortly afterwards classical music filtered out into the bedroom. The music stopped as suddenly as it started. When Brian came out, he snickered. "You'll never guess what happens when you sit on the throne."

***

Brian returned from the meeting shortly after five. As he left his business associate's car, his eyes were drawn to the second floor window where his bride, seated next to a gaily sequined mannequin, smiled and waved.

A few seconds later she met him at the door of their room and enveloped him with her arms holding him close, closer than she had since the wedding. Goose bumps spread down his arms and a tingling feeling made its way around the rest of his body. He lingered there, enjoying the closeness with her. He'd planned to apologize for working on their honeymoon, but she seemed so happy, he didn't want to say anything to break the spell.

She appeared to be in no hurry to let go of him either, but eventually she pushed back gently with her eyes locked on his. She had a glow on her face he hadn't seen since the day the subpoena was delivered.

"How did your meeting go?" she asked.

Brian let her go long enough to close the door and walk into the main part of the room with her. He showed her a manila envelope. "Got the contract right here, signed for another five years. Just what we need to stay competitive."

"Wonderful. You ready to celebrate?"

"Of course," he said, wondering what she had in mind. Whatever it was, she made it sound exciting.

"I talked to Tea while you were gone and she told me where we should go to eat. Plus, she gave us a coupon for a free meal."

"Coupon?" Brian asked. He hadn't needed or used a coupon for, well, never.

"I know what you're thinking. Quit it. Just because we can afford it, we can take a free meal when it's offered. Don't be a snob."

Was she concerned about the lawsuit and trying to save money because of the possibility of a large payout? Was she happy or was she acting like she was happy for him? Why didn't he know?

"We should be good stewards at all times," she said, "no matter how much money we have. I know how you and Phil help college students with books and tuition. Just think of using a coupon as a way to have more to give away."

He kissed her on the cheek and laughed as he walked away, loosening his tie. "Okay. I get it. So, tell me about this place Tea recommended."

"In addition to managing this place and studying to be an artist, Tea works as a waitress at a barbeque place near here." Karen held up a piece of paper with red, white and blue writing on it. "With this coupon we get all-we-can-eat ribs for two for the price of one."

He looked at the coupon. "Texas Ribs? That's the name of the place?"

"That's right."

Brian was disappointed. They could get Texas food at home. He'd wanted to try the local fare, but Karen sounded excited about going to the place where Tea worked. "When do you want to go."

She looked at her watch. "How about now?"

Brian tossed the envelope on the breakfast table, where a mannequin stared at it. "I'm ready. In fact, I'm starved."

The restaurant was close by. Brian was glad he didn't have to drive. He'd decided to return the car to the rental agency, and didn't want to have to drive in town again. Maybe the rental people could come get it. Brian's nose perked up and his mind switched gears when they were a block away from the restaurant. He recognized the smell of burning wood and the special spices rubbed into ribs. It reminded him of Rudy's back in Austin. He winked at Karen, and picked up the pace.

He'd fallen in love with Texas smoked meats while a student at the University of Texas. Could a place in Belgium compete with what he was used to?

Texas Ribs was a small white building on the corner of two streets as narrow and cobbled as the others they had seen in Bruges. Even so, several cars were parked on the sidewalk, leaving little room for pedestrians, much less other vehicles. The structure was older than dirt and, as they entered, Brian chuckled when he saw it had an actual dirt floor.

Tea waved at them from across the room and pointed to a table in back next to the grill. The long room was narrow, but cavernous. The grill sat on top of a rock foundation with a huge chimney to take away the smoke. The cook wasn't slow-cooking the ribs the way they did in Texas. He grilled them directly on the wood fire, making Brian wonder if the meat would be tender enough to enjoy. At least a dozen racks sizzled on the grill, the smell floating around Karen and Brian's table.

"Evening," the cook said, waving his tongs in the air. "Glad you could come tonight. Tea tells me you're from Texas."

"We are," Brian said. "But not originally. I moved there from California and Karen grew up in Iowa. She's lived in Texas for more than thirty years, though. Most people consider her to be a native Texan."

"Good. I'd like to know what you think of my ribs. I want to know how they compare to those you get back home."

Brian hoped he could be honest about the meal without hurting the man's feelings, but he had his doubts about that. "Sure will," he said.

The aisle to the restrooms was between the grill and their table. Everyone seemed to know who they were and that they were from Texas. Tea must have spread the news to all the patrons. Most stopped to chat and some said hello as they passed by on their way to the toilets.

Not everyone was friendly, though. One man stood out because of his silence. He didn't go to the restroom the whole time they were there. Brian couldn't see the man's face, but from the shape of his body and the back of his head he had a funny feeling he'd seen the man before.

It wasn't long before the cook delivered two racks of bubbling-hot ribs to their table and plopped them on a piece of brown butcher paper, one for each of them. Tea brought plates covered with beans, coleslaw, pickles, and onions. Barbeque sauce and sliced bread stood ready for them as well.

The meat didn't look appetizing. The fatty parts were black. Some of the bone tips were also charred. Brian had never eaten anything that large in a single sitting in his life and he was sure he'd be expected to. Leaving too much meat on the table would be an insult to the cook.

"Look at the size of this thing," Karen said, leaning in close to him to whisper. "I'll never be able to eat all of this."

Brian smiled. "Me neither. We should have asked for half a rack each."

It pleased him to see her happy. Looking at her made him want to leave this strange-looking meat on the table and take her in his arms. He wanted to carry her back to their room full of mannequins.

Karen took a bite and popped her eyes . "Wait until you try this," she said. Blackened grease and red velvet sauce decorated her cheek. She licked her fingers and pulled another rib off the rack.

After the first bite, Brian knew he could, indeed, eat the whole thing. It was the best meat he'd ever put in his mouth, and so tender he could cut it with a fork. Brian gave the cook a greasy thumbs up and forked off another piece of meat. The cook smiled and tossed more meat onto the grill.

They ate with gusto. Karen hadn't eaten nearly as much meat as he had, but she sampled the sides while Brian ate mostly ribs. Just as he got to the last one, and was proud of doing so, the cook plunked another large one on the table in front of him.

"Whoa," Brian said. "One's enough."

"Oh, no. You're Texan. Surely you can eat two or three."

Brian held up his sticky hands palm up and shrugged. Can't hurt the man's feelings.

***

They waddled out of the Texas Ribs two hours after getting there, and walked hand in hand admiring the July sky. Stars shone brightly overhead. When they got to a bridge overlooking the canal they stopped. Brian pulled Karen close and held her in his arms. A long passionate kiss followed. She tasted like barbeque sauce, but he was sure he did, too. When they finally came up for air, they moved in unison toward their bed and breakfast, holding hands again, while walking with purpose.

In their room, they quickly closed the door and continued the kiss began at the canal. Karen stood back and unbuttoned her blouse as Brian watched. But the mannequins observed, as well. They both laughed, becoming aware of their audience at the same time. Karen turned the mannequin next to the bed so that it faced the other direction. Brian turned off the bedroom lights, and closed the bathroom door part way, leaving a glow of light shining in from there.

And then the thirty years apart was forever forgotten.

Love Lives On

Afterwards, Brian held Karen in his arms, telling her how much he loved her. He had no regrets about the past because he knew he would be with her for the rest of their lives. He was at peace. And, so sleepy...

Judy pointed at him in a mall, somewhere in California. "Hey, I know you. Brad, right?"

"Brian."

"Come here. I remember you from high school."

"Amy? What are you doing here?"

"I'm not your real daughter, you know. But you'll always be my father."

The mall turned into the steep rooftop of the Texas Ribs in Bruges, except the building was much taller. He was alone now, and about to fall. His body dangled down the side of the ten-story building and the only thing that kept him from plummeting to his death was a single slate roof shingle more than a hundred years old that was gradually flaking apart.

CHAPTER SEVEN

"Brian! Wake up." Karen tightened the sash around her robe to ward off the early morning chill. She sat next to him on the bed and kissed his forehead. "Are you okay?" she asked, looking into his eyes. "You were mumbling so loud and acting upset I had to wake you."

Brian sat up and covered himself with the sheet. "I dreamed something about Judy, but I don't remember what."

"Well, I'm glad I woke you if you were dreaming about your ex-wife."

"No, nothing like that. If anything, it was a nightmare. I'm glad you helped end it."

Karen smiled to let him know she wasn't concerned about Judy. "I made tea. Want some?"

"Sure. Just what I need." He rubbed his eyes and brushed his hair back. "What time is it?"

"It's a few minutes past midnight." She couldn't resist kissing his sleepy head. "I woke up and couldn't get back to sleep. I finally gave up and made some tea. I guess it's the time change."

He put on a white terry cloth robe and joined her at the table. Karen poured his tea.

Brian took a sip and replaced the cup on the saucer. "I'm sorry about ruining our honeymoon with work. I know you had your mind set on visiting Hildesheim and we were only there for one night. Now that I've done what needs to be done in Bruges, we can go back to Germany tomorrow if you like."

She was silent for a few seconds as she remembered Hildesheim. "Let's stay here for the rest of our honeymoon."

The temperature in the room was comfortable, but her hands were shaking. She cupped them around the tea, drawing in its warmth. Was it Brian's dream? Was it the lawsuit worry creeping back into her consciousness?

"I suggested Hildesheim for a honeymoon since you talked about it so much. I knew you loved it and I wanted to share that with you. But, it's your place, not ours. I didn't realize that until we got here."

She motioned around the room. "This crazy place with all these weird characters and strange surroundings. This is our place. The funny town we got lost in. The place where we found the best ribs in the world. The place where we made love."

Brian's face reflected what had to be joy, making his blue eyes sparkle more than usual.

She wished she was as happy as he seemed. "This is our special place. A place I'll never forget."

Brian's grin grew as she spoke, and when she looked close she could see his eyes were damp. "Bruges will always be special to me, too," he said. His voice cracked as he spoke and she loved him all the more.

He turned away, but couldn't hide the paper napkin he used to dab his eyes.

"Every time I visited this town they put me up in some fancy hotel that reminded me of any other large hotel in the world. And not once did I walk along the canal with a gorgeous woman or eat ribs like a starving man. I never saw a room full of dummies."

He turned to the mannequin sitting at the table with them. "Sorry, ma'am. And I never felt so loved in a foreign country, or anywhere else in the world for that matter."

Karen smiled, forcing herself to maintain the positive face she wanted to have.

Brian took her hand and squeezed it lovingly. "So, I guess this is, and always will be, our special place."

"Good. There's more to see, too. Besides finding a great place to eat, I talked to Tea about what we should do while we're in town. We've got a full day of touristy stuff lined up for tomorrow." She checked the clock on the table next to the bed. "Or later today, to be accurate."

"Wonderful. I thought you were unhappy in Germany because of the lawsuit."

Karen felt a kick in the gut she didn't expect, and didn't want. It must have shone on her face.

"I'm sorry," Brian said, shaking his head. "That was a stupid thing for me to say."

"No. It's okay. If we can't talk about it, they win." She set her tea cup on the saucer and walked to the window. It was dark outside and quieter than the night they spent on the market square in Hildesheim. A breeze rushed through the open window and brushed against her face. She didn't want the lawsuit to take over her life, but her feelings about it were out of her control.

She turned to Brian. "To be honest, thinking about the lawsuit hurts. I start to obsess about it and want to know why God has given me this burden. Even so, I'm determined to not let it mess up our honeymoon. I'm doing my best to save all the worrying for when we get back to Texas."

Brian stood and came to her. "I'm sorry. I just didn't think."

"I'm okay." She allowed his arms to surround her and comfort her, knowing the security she felt was temporary. She'd have to face her accusers when she got back home. She pushed him away gently and gave him a kiss on the cheek. "Do you think you could get some more sleep? We'll need it if we're going to do all the things on the list for tomorrow."

They got back in bed, but didn't go to sleep right away. Afterwards, Brian slept but Karen stayed awake wondering why God had decided she needed a lawsuit in her life. Especially now, back in the arms of the one person she'd ever loved. The last thing she remembered before falling asleep was how she wished she'd never met Ernest Brower.

***

Brian slipped out of bed with first light, careful not to wake Karen. He showered and dressed quietly, letting her sleep as long as she wanted. He was ready to start the day for the first time in years. He didn't want to miss a second of his new life with Karen. He searched for the manila envelope that held the new contract so he could put it away, but he couldn't find it. A gentle knock on the door reminded him they had ordered an early breakfast. When he opened the door, Tea was placing a tray of food on the small table in the hallway.

"Good morning," he said.

She smiled. "Good morning. Didn't know if you two were up yet. Gotta go get breakfast for the other guests. Enjoy." She turned and ran down the stairs.

He picked up the tray and placed it on the dining table. One plastic-wrapped plate was stacked high with a variety of cheeses and sliced meats. A basket lined with a red and white-checkered cloth napkin contained rolls. Round, oblong, brown, white, all tasty-looking. The coffee was in a push-down pot, the plunger handle riding high. A plastic bucket of spreadable butter and three small glass jars of fruit jams took up the rest of the space on the shiny black plastic tray.

He kissed Karen gently on the forehead. "Sorry to wake you, but breakfast is here."

She opened one eye partway, its eyebrow raised.

"Remember," he said, "we asked Tea to bring breakfast at seven this morning so we'd have more time to be tourists?"

Karen closed the eye. He kissed her on the forehead again.

"It was your idea, actually," he said.

Karen sat up with both eyes opened this time. She stretched. "Oh, I know. I'm sort of awake. I was having a wonderful dream. I didn't want it to end."

"I'm sorry. Do you want to go back to sleep? It's a cold breakfast. Except for the coffee."

"No, I'm awake now."

"Good. I'll meet you at the table."

"In my nightgown?"

"Of course. You look magnificent."

She smiled, and he reluctantly turned away to get breakfast ready. He pushed the coffee pot plunger. The smell of fresh coffee wafted around the room. That was all it took to get her out of bed.

"Mmm. I'll have some of that. But let me at least comb my hair." Karen went into the bathroom and closed the door.

When she was back, he poured them both a cup and lifted the plastic wrap off the cheese and meat. "Look at the breads," he said pulling back the napkin covering them.

"I can't believe I'm hungry again after that feast last night," she said reaching for the whole wheat oblong roll he'd eyed. He hadn't had time to select another before she tore hers apart and handed him half.

"Thanks," he said. "How'd you know I wanted that one?"

She laughed. "You were drooling."

"No I wasn't," he said, laughing.

He popped the lid off the butter and opened the jams.

"You didn't happen to see that contract I showed you yesterday, did you?" he asked as they continued to eat.

"I saw it on this table before we went out for dinner."

Brian picked up the tray and looked under it, knowing nothing was there. "That's where I put it."

"Are you sure you didn't put it in your suitcase?"

He stood.

"Don't you want to finish breakfast first?"

"It'll just take a second." He unzipped his suitcase and looked in. It was empty. He searched the rest of the room and the bathroom. No envelope. He sat down at the table to finish breakfast, wondering where it could be.

"What happens if it's lost?" she asked.

"Nothing. I'm sure they'll send me another. It's just that I don't know where it could be. It means someone may have come into the room while we were gone."

"I guess Tea could have."

"Yes, but she was at the restaurant when we got there and when we left. We didn't go straight back to the room, though." He took a bite of a roll with a slice of cheese on it.

"Honey, there's something I didn't tell you yesterday."

"What's that?"

"When we first got here, you were parking the car while I was standing out front of the bed and breakfast, I saw a guy peeking around the corner of a building. He was watching us, but trying to stay concealed. I assumed it was just a curious neighbor. After spotting that photographer in Hildesheim, I wonder if someone searched our room."

"I guess it's possible. Doesn't seem likely though. Maybe the maid tossed the envelope in the trash by mistake."

"I think Tea does her own cleaning. We'll ask her before we leave."

He pushed away from the table, shaken about the envelope. "We better look around to see if anything else is missing."

Karen wiped her mouth and dropped the black napkin on the table. "You're right."

They searched the bedroom, bathroom and both their suitcases. Brian didn't find anything missing.

"Uh-oh," Karen said sitting on the bed. "My ring's gone."

"Your wedding ring?"

"No. I haven't taken my engagement ring or my wedding ring off. It's my Alpha Omega ring."

"Are you sure?" His heart sank. They had matching rings bought more than thirty years ago. The date they first went out back in college was engraved in the wide gold with the Greek letters Alpha and Omega, the beginning and the end. He hadn't lost his, but he couldn't help looking at his right hand.

"I took it off yesterday and put it on the lamp table here. It's gone."

"Did you look in the jewelry bag you carry in your purse?" he asked.

"Yes. It's not there."

They searched everywhere without finding the ring, but found nothing more missing.

"Okay," Brian said. "Let's talk to Tea and see what she suggests. We might need to call the police. It's sad to lose the ring, but luckily it's replaceable. Yours looked almost new since you had stored it away until fairly recently."

"I loved that ring, though. A new one wouldn't be the same."

"I know. We'll do what we can to get it back, but there's a distinct possibility we'll never see it again. I suggest we not let its loss ruin the rest of our time here. If we do, the crooks will have taken more from us than a ring."

"You're right," she said.

Brian called Tea and told her what had happened. She apologized profusely. She hadn't cleaned the room yet, but planned to do so today while we were out. She also said as far as she knows, nothing had ever been stolen in her place before. She said she would notify the police just in case. She confessed that the doors are often unlocked since home thefts are rare. Brian relayed the information to Karen.

"Okay. Let's enjoy our time here. What's first on the agenda for the tourists today?"

"We don't have particular times for any of the activities and places Tea told me about. However, I'd like to go to the market square first. There's a belfry tower that's supposed to have a remarkable view of the city. After we take that in, we can look around and decide what we want to do next."

Karen picked up her notebook. "While we're in the square, Tea said to be sure and see the statues of Jan Breydel and Pieter de Coninck, two of their national heroes." She read her notes. "They led an uprising against the French back in the 1300s. Breydel's so famous there's a football stadium named after him. He was a butcher and de Coninck was a weaver."

"Okay," he said. "We go to the market square, look out the belfry, and visit the famous statues. What next?"

"Tea said a visit to the Basilica of the Holy Blood is a must."

"What's that?" he asked.

"It's a Catholic church built in the twelfth century. Originally it was the chapel for the Count of Flanders. A cloth there is supposed to have the blood of Jesus on it."

"That sounds interesting," Brian said.

"Sometime today, I'd like to take the boat tour. Did you know Bruges is called the Venice of the North?" Karen picked up a brochure. "Tea gave me this. It says the Reie River was dredged to prevent flooding from the North Sea. That resulted in a network of canals running through the town. We can take a boat ride and hear more about the sights."

"That sounds like fun," he said.

Brian hoped touring Bruges would keep her mind off the theft and the lawsuit, but he'd have to be careful not to bring it up again. He couldn't help wondering what'd happened to the contract and her ring.

They got to the market square, saw the statues, and climbed up to the belfry tower for the view. After that they saw a convent where they learned the movie *The Nun's Story* was filmed and watched some women make lace. Next, they joined a tour group to see and hear about the inside of the church. The guide made the tour fun and interesting. He wasn't sure when it happened, but one minute he was holding Karen's hand and listening to the history of the church and the next minute his hand was empty. Karen had vanished.

CHAPTER EIGHT

He found her sitting on the third row of pews with her arm around a woman old enough to be her mother. The woman stared at the altar. Her gray hair flared out in strange places.

Brian sat next to Karen. "Is your friend okay?"

"I'm not sure. She may be in shock. Let me talk to her and see what I can find out."

"Okay, but what about the tour?"

"Tour? Oh, we can do that anytime." She turned from Brian toward the woman next to her.

Brian remembered how Karen had used her Stephen Ministry training to help friends and family. She'd told him about the classes she'd taken to become a Stephen Minister. She helped women in the church with short-term problems. From time to time she used that knowledge and experience in other places, primarily at school. In the past year, one of her students and the student's mother lived at Karen's house for a while to keep them away from an abusive man. A pregnant teenager lived there, too, for a short time. Karen had a knack for spotting people in need and she knew how to help. As he watched her now, he saw a spark that had been missing since the lawsuit had been filed.

Brian found the tour guide and told her they'd have to leave the tour. He slipped her a few euros as he shook her hand and complimented her on what he'd heard of her talk.

He scooted into the pew next to Karen. He didn't want to intrude, but he wanted to be close in case she needed him. The woman seemed calmer now and Brian could easily hear her responses to Karen's questions.

"My name is Karen Donelson and this is my husband Brian. What's your name?"

"Harriet Boyles," the woman said with a whimper, and an accent like Liz's.

"Where are you from?" Karen asked.

"Asheville. This is my first time outside of No'th Carolina. My husband didn't care to travel, you see. After he died last year, the kids got together and gave me this trip. Now, I've messed it up." Her snivel turned into a full-fledged sob.

Brian handed Karen his handkerchief and she passed it to Harriet. The woman dabbed both eyes. "Thank you," she said.

Karen patted her on the back. "What happened? How did you mess things up?"

The woman blew her nose. "My purse. I lost my purse. All my money, credit cards, passport. Even my cell phone. Everything's gone." She said it with strength.

"Did someone take your purse?"

"I can't honestly say. I don't know if somebody stole it or if I sat it down somewhere and forgot it. All I know is it's gone."

"Don't worry. It happens all the time. This can be fixed."

"No," Harriet said. "The tour guide said if we lose our passport we're off the tour and on our own to get back home." She cried out loud. "I...I don't know how to do that."

"Did you talk to your tour guide after you lost your purse?" Karen asked.

"Why? She told us what would happen."

"Sometimes they say that just so people will be more careful. Surely, the tour company will help."

The woman's eyes opened wide. "Really? I didn't think of that. Why would they want to scare us so?" She bawled louder.

"Where is your group now?" Karen asked.

"Gone," Harriet sniffed loudly, and blew her nose again. "They're gone. Should be in Oberammergau by now. That's all the way to Germany somewhere. They went without me, I'm sure."

"Oh, dear," Karen said. "Don't you fret, we can figure out what to do." She turned to Brian. "We're going to need some local assistance. Will you call your business associates and ask if someone could meet us at that bakery we saw on the market square? I think Harriet could use a bite to eat."

Brian smiled as he watched Harriet's face light up. "Sure," he said.

By the time Harriet finished her sandwich and they all had a cup of coffee, Brian's Bruges contact had joined them. Pieter Sybesma was a tall, slender man with curly black hair beginning to thin. He wore a black suit with a white dress shirt and thin black tie. After introductions and an explanation of the problem, Pieter said he'd take care of everything.

"Harriet," Brian said, looking her in the eye and waiting until she focused on him, "you can trust this man. Pieter will help you report your missing purse to the police and he'll assist you in getting a new passport. I bet he'll find you a place to stay. If you want to rejoin your tour group he can help you do that when the time comes. Otherwise, he'll help you find a flight home."

Harriet stared at Brian in disbelief before she turned to Pieter. "You can do all that?"

"Not to worry, madam," Pieter said. "You can count on me."

Karen reached into her purse and pulled out a wad of euros. She handed the cash to Harriet. "Here, take this."

Harriet pushed her hand away. "I couldn't."

"This is just a loan," Karen said. "You can repay me when you get back to the states. If you need more while you're here, call us." She gave her one of Brian's business cards with his cell phone number on it.

"You'll need this, too," Karen said as she handed Harriet her cell phone.

"Your phone?" Harriet's eyes nearly popped out.

"Yes. If anyone calls for me, tell them to call Brian's number. It's on that card I gave you."

"But…" Harriet seemed to be at a loss for words.

"It's okay," Karen said. "Call your children right away and tell them where you are and that you're okay. Just in case they try to call you or the tour company you were traveling with."

"Yes," Harriet said, looking better now. "I didn't think of that. I better call home right away. My son has phoned me every day and he's probably trying to track me down right now. He has my itinerary."

Harriet hugged Karen, Brian and Pieter, one after the other. "You're all so kind. I don't know what I would have done if you hadn't been here to help." She looked Karen in the eye. "Bless you."

"Someone else would have helped," Karen said. "You call us if you need anything at all."

"I will," Harriet said.

"Thanks, Pieter," Brian whispered. "Take good care of Harriet. I'll reimburse you for all the expenses."

"Will she be okay?" Karen asked Brian after Harriet and Pieter left.

"Sure," he said. "Pieter is the head of the legal department. She'll be just fine. So, what do you want to do next? Sightseeing-wise, that is."

Karen eyed her watch. "We have time to catch the boat tour."

They joined the excursion at a stop behind the church, not far from the market square. The boat held about thirty people and it was full. The guide described the historical views around the canal in English and Dutch while adding stories about what they were seeing. He showed where the Colin Farrell movie, *In Bruges,* was filmed. At one point they approached a rock bridge that had probably been there for a thousand years. The bridge and the surrounding area reminded Brian of a painting. As Brian was immersed in the beauty of the bridge and its surroundings, he saw a young man with a camera standing on the bridge with his long-lens camera pointed toward the boat. Brian thought the man might be taking photos of tourists to sell to them at the end of the tour. He'd seen that tactic used in many places. But just before the boat went under the bridge, he saw that the photographer was the same person Karen had pointed out to him in Hildesheim.

Brian turned to Karen to see if she saw him, too. She pointed her camera toward the church, away from the bridge.

"Karen," he started to call her attention to the photographer.

"Just a minute," she said. "Let me take this. What a beautiful view."

He heard her camera click.

"Yes it is." His head told him to insist on her attention. To show her what he'd seen. But he didn't.

Finding the same young man in the white tee shirt that didn't fit and the same English driving cap taking photos of them here in Bruges was too bizarre. Telling her would worry her and steal time from her vacation.

They enjoyed another week of sightseeing and dining in Bruges and Brian didn't see the photographer again, even though he searched for him everywhere they went. By the time they were on the plane headed home, he'd convinced himself it was better not to mention what he'd seen on the bridge over the canal in Bruges.

CHAPTER NINE

Brian and Karen didn't take the bookmobile out for two weeks after they returned from their honeymoon. Liz provided a driver and librarian to keep the mobile library on schedule. Brian met with Ron to talk about the business. He went over the financial reports and got caught up on operations for the California company. The Bruges company had mailed a signed copy of the contract to replace the one stolen from the bed and breakfast.

Karen met with Richard to discuss her lawsuit. He said nothing had happened since she'd departed for her honeymoon, but he'd start pushing the plaintiffs more now that she was back home.

Karen spent much of the rest of her time off at her Sunset Valley home, moving odds and ends to her new home with Brian. She hoped to eventually sell the house, but wasn't in a hurry since Julie lived there when she wasn't staying at Amy's condo near the University.

On the first Thursday after their time off, Karen and Brian parked the bookmobile in the strip mall near Clarksville and set up for business. She went through the motions, but all she could think about was the case. She'd felt better in Belgium, even though she worried about the lawsuit more than she'd let on to Brian.

What was wrong with her? She'd never been a negative person. Her mother taught her early on to make lemonade out of lemons and she'd lived her life looking on the bright side of everything thrown her way. She knew all the clichés about being positive. Even so, she had begun to feel she was the victim in this lawsuit and she had no control over its outcome. She needed to quit wallowing in self-pity. Liz had never sat around doing nothing when she'd been the bookmobile librarian. She went out in the parking lot recruiting customers if she had to. Or she dusted and cleaned. Liz didn't sit still. Even now, in her desk job as head of library services, she could sometimes be seen walking the aisles straightening books and cleaning shelves.

Karen sat in the forward librarian chair thinking about the lawsuit and why God had given her such a heavy burden at the same time she was starting a new life with Brian. She'd prayed all her life for a loving relationship like the one she now had. Her prayers were answered when Brian came back into her life, but as long as she was accused of something she didn't do, she couldn't think about anything else. God knew how precious Brian was to her and how the lawsuit would affect her. The only answer was that God had a purpose for giving her both trouble and blessing at the same time. The reason eluded her.

Brian didn't seem to have a problem working this morning. Like Liz, he loved a neat library. He pulled books forward on the shelves to line up the spines and dusted while she sat staring into space.

When she wasn't obsessing about the lawsuit, she thought about Judy. That dream Brian told her about in Bruges bothered her more than she'd said. Not that she was worried about Judy, but she was reminded of the way Brian had reacted when he'd learned Judy was expecting. He'd married Judy out of what—guilt, obligation? Brian didn't tell himself God must have a purpose for him. No. Brian had blamed God, dropped out of church and hadn't gone back for thirty years.

The only way she could get past the pain of this frivolous lawsuit was to believe God had a reason for it. A purpose that would eventually lead to something worthy of its cost, both financially and emotionally. She didn't care if the benefits were for her or someone else. She'd always believed God's plans were perfectly timed.

So, how should she react otherwise? God didn't want her to take abuse from anyone, not even Ernest's ex-wife and his son. God wanted her to be assertive and to do what was right to take care of herself and her loved ones. But, what? What did God want of her in this situation?

"Oh, I forgot to ask. What did Harriet say when she called this morning?" Brian asked.

Karen smiled, remembering the conversation she'd had with the woman from North Carolina they'd helped in Bruges.

"She's doing fine. In fact, she called to tell me she's off on another tour."

"Really? Where to this time?" Brian held a crazy-looking yellow and black feathered duster and flipped it across the tops of the books and bare shelves.

"She's going to Ireland."

"Ireland?" Brian sounded surprised. "I guess she learned it's possible to survive the theft of a purse. When I first saw her sitting in that church next to you, I thought for sure she was going to pass out."

Karen shook her head. "I think she was in shock."

"What about your cell phone? Did she say anything about it?"

"Yes. She mailed it, along with the money we loaned her. She wanted to make sure she sent it before she left town again."

"I'm glad to hear she's not afraid of traveling after what happened in Bruges."

"Me, too. Oh, and she said to check the voice mail on the phone. She listened to it thinking it was for her. But it mentions my name. She said the message wasn't nice."

"Really?"

A young man climbed aboard the bookmobile. Brian turned and walked to the back of the library, stopping to dust books as he went.

"Howdy, ma'am," the man said. He wore jeans with a cowboy belt that went under his stomach instead of around his waist. The tee shirt would've covered more of his "inner tube" if it were a few sizes larger.

"Come in," Karen said. He seemed familiar, but she couldn't think why. Probably because he looked like most of the college-aged young men she saw at church.

He walked to the center of the vehicle, near the biographies, and examined the spines. He pulled out a book and opened it. Brian was at the rear of the library jiggling the air conditioner switches. When Brian turned toward Karen he had a funny look on his face., The look turned to a scowl as he walked quickly toward the patron.

"You! What are you doing here?" he shouted. His face was red and he looked and acted agitated.

Karen looked at the visitor again, trying to identify him. "What's the matter?" she asked Brian.

The young man stood frozen in place for a second or two with the book still in his hand. "I just want to borrow a book."

"You're lying," Brian moved closer to the young man.

"Should I call the police?" Karen asked.

The patron looked scared. Brian ignored the question. He stopped a foot away from the young man, leaned in, his eyes wide open, fists clenched at his sides. "Who are you working for?"

"What's your problem, dude?" he asked as he backed up against the bookshelf.

"What do you want?" Brian asked. "Did someone pay you to stalk us? Who? Why?"

The book the man had held made a slapping sound as it hit the floor. He pushed Brian away and ran out the front door.

Brian followed him to the parking lot.

Karen went out, too, and grabbed Brian by the arm. She had never seen him angry, and could tell he wanted to chase the man. "No, don't run after him. I want to know what's going on."

They stood together frozen in place until the young man ran behind the grocery store. Only then did she relax her hold on Brian.

"He got away," Brian said.

"What's going on?" she repeated. "Should we call the police or not? What'd he do? I didn't see what happened."

Brian wouldn't make eye contact at first, but when he finally did, he stared at her for what seemed like minutes. The frown he'd worn since the stranger appeared slowly dissolved. When he spoke, she could hardly hear him.

"What?" she asked.

"I said, that was the photographer you saw in Hildesheim at the bakery shop."

Karen turned toward the corner of the store where the young man had been. "What? That was him? I thought I recognized him."

"It was him."

"How do you know? You saw him from the back. Maybe it's someone who looks like him, with similar clothes. It would be unlikely for him to be in Germany and here, too."

"It was him. I'm sure." Brian kept his gaze on Karen.

"How can you say that? Is there something you're not telling me?"

"I saw him in Bruges, too. I saw his face there. I was close enough to reach out and touch him."

"In Bruges?" Karen hadn't seen him there.

"Yes."

"You didn't tell me?"

Brian turned his head down for a second before looking her straight in the eyes again. "No. I'm sorry. I didn't want to upset you. At first I wasn't certain it was him. It happened during the canal boat tour. I didn't have the heart to dampen your spirits."

"I can't believe you. What else are you hiding to protect me?" Karen turned away from Brian. She climbed in the bookmobile, repositioned her seat and buckled up, ready to travel.

He followed her into the mobile library. "Nothing," he said. "It wasn't just that. I didn't have enough information to be sure. I thought he might be the same guy, but it wasn't until today that I knew for sure."

"I'm sorry," she said. "I'm just angry. Please don't try to protect me. I can take care of myself. I've done okay alone for a long time. If you had told me we could have decided together if it was or wasn't the same person. The young man must have something to do with the lawsuit. Is that what you're thinking? Is that why you didn't tell me?"

"I guess," he said. "That's what I thought in Bruges. Now I'm not sure. Remember what Amy said about her mother? Judy may have sent this guy to spy on me."

"Why would your ex-wife send someone to Germany, Belgium, and now Texas to spy on us?"

"I don't know. Amy wasn't sure what her mom was going to do. Judy has threatened to sue for more alimony before."

"I guess it's possible. I still think the young man you scared off is somehow connected to my lawsuit," Karen said.

Brian took her hands in his. "I'm sorry I didn't tell you about my suspicions in Bruges. Maybe if I had, you could have helped me watch the guy. Now, because of me, he knows we're on to him. That's going to make it harder to find him."

She was silent.

"We need to find out who this guy is and why he's following us. I'll ask Ron to track him down."

"I thought Ron was your accountant."

"He is, but he's the one I called on when I set out to find you. I'll ask him tomorrow at the Combine lunch."

"Okay, but you've got to promise me not to hold back information just because it might hurt me to hear it."

"I promise. I just got caught up in the situation and by the time I knew I should say something, it was too late."

"It's never too late. Just talk to me. We both have a long history of secrets and the only way we got back together was with honesty and openness."

"I understand. I'm sorry."

CHAPTER TEN

The next day, Brian drove alone to Phil's house where the Combine was getting together for a barbeque. Karen had gone to the movies with the other wives but they'd be there in time for dinner. As he pulled into the Clarksville neighborhood where Phil and Kay lived, his mind was on Karen and the young stalker they'd encountered. He didn't understand why she wanted to go through the trial when they were able to give the plaintiffs the money they wanted. Still, he would leave that decision to her.

He pulled up to the curb near the house. Richard and Matt's cars were parked in front. Ron was the one he needed to talk to and his car wasn't there. He would probably arrive shortly. Brian wanted to ask him about a private detective to find out who was stalking them.

Tony's car wasn't there, either, but that was to be expected. He'd be missing a lot of meetings for a while since he'd moved to New York to try his hand in the entertainment business.

Brian started to knock on the front door, but he got a whiff of Texas-style barbeque sauce and the smell of burning wood. He followed his nose and found the guys in the backyard.

"Hey, Brian's here." Phil wore a black smock with large red letters claiming 'Real Men Wear Aprons' while holding tongs smeared with barbeque sauce as dark as the color of raw calf liver.

Brian walked toward the smoker with his nose high as if following the scent.

Phil laughed. "I knew you'd find us here. The smell is driving my neighbors crazy. We may have to feed the bunch of 'em."

Brian hugged all his friends and thanked God for having them in his life.

"Is your dad here?" Brian asked Phil. Brian always liked to talk to George. He'd been the one who had helped Brian most to regain his trust in God.

"Naw. He's over at the church working on some landscaping. I'm supposed to be there, too." He smiled. "I'm using you guys as my excuse."

"Oh."

"Don't look so upset. He'll be here for dinner."

"Well there you are," Ron said. "I rang the front doorbell forever."

"Sorry," Phil replied. "Everyone else smelled us back here."

He sniffed the air. "Oh, yeah. Duh."

"I need to talk to you, Ron," Brian said.

"Okay." He shook hands with all. "What's up? Need me to do some more private detective work?" Ron pulled two root beers out the ice bucket and handed one to Brian.

"As a matter of fact," Brian said, "that's exactly what I need."

"Oh, no," Richard said. "His head never got back down to normal size after helping you find Karen. Don't get him started again."

"Yeah," Matt said. "He tells us every time we see him how he's responsible for you and Karen getting back together."

Brian smiled. "I know. I'm sorry guys, but I need to ask Ron about business. Someone is following me or Karen or both of us, and I wondered if it has anything to do with the company. Have you heard any rumblings from the previous owners, Ron? Or it may be someone Judy hired or something to do with Karen's lawsuit."

"Wait a minute," Phil said. "What do you mean you're being followed?"

"Tell us," Matt said. "What's going on?"

His friends moved in closer waiting for what he had to say.

"There's this young kid, probably twenty or twenty-five. He's taller than me, so maybe six-three or four. He's stout. Actually, chubby around the waist."

His friends listened quietly, not making jokes the way they'd done when he'd moved back to Austin and told them he was going to get Karen to fall in love with him again.

"We noticed him in Germany while we were sitting at an outdoor table having coffee. Karen's the one who saw him first. She insisted he'd pointed a camera at us, but I never saw it. By the time I looked where she was pointing, he was walking away. He wore jeans, white tee shirt and an English driving cap that you know didn't belong on his head."

"What'd you do?" Ron asked.

"Do? We didn't do anything. I assumed he was some kook who liked to take photos of attractive women. Maybe sell them on the Internet or something. I don't know. Karen found it curious, but didn't seem to be concerned."

"So why do you think he's following you?" Matt asked.

"Because he showed up in Bruges." Brian said.

"That's in Belgium." Ron said. "I made all the travel arrangements."

"Yes. We went there to sign some papers for my company, and to continue our honeymoon, of course."

"You saw the same guy in Bruges?" Richard asked. "You're sure?"

"Positive. We were on a boat tour on the canal there. He stood in the center of one of the bridges. As the boat began to go under the bridge, he snapped our photos. At that point, I was close enough to reach out and touch him. Now, I wish I had. I heard his camera click. It was him. Same build, same clothes, same hat."

"What'd you think was happening?" Phil asked.

"We were being followed. No question about it."

"Did you call the cops?" Phil asked.

"No. What would I tell the police?

"You could have called Pieter," Ron said.

"Who's that?" Matt asked.

"Pieter's our contact at the automated brush manufacturing company there."

"I'd talked to Pieter earlier in the day on another matter, but I didn't think he could do anything about someone taking pictures of us."

"What'd Karen think?" Richard asked.

Brian took a sip of root beer before answering. "I didn't tell her."

"What?" Matt said. He was the quiet one in the group, not the one Brian expected to respond to his confession about not telling Karen.

"I know I should have," Brian said. "But at the time I only wanted to protect her, and let her enjoy the honeymoon."

"You need to tell her," Matt said.

"I did. Eventually. There's more to this story."

"Wait a minute," Phil said. He turned to the smoker, opened the lid on the burn-box and added two logs to the fire. The delicious smell of ribs surrounded them again. Phil returned. "Okay. Now you can continue. You said there's more? What happened?"

"The kid came aboard the bookmobile yesterday."

"What? He's in Germany, Belgium, and now here?" Ron's voice was louder now; concerned.

"Yes. It wasn't until he showed up there that I knew we had a problem."

"What happened?" Richard asked.

"Well, we parked near here," Brian said, pointing over his head. "In the Clarksville shopping center there. We'd had few patrons so there wasn't much to do. I was dusting the shelves and Karen was sitting at the front desk when this same guy walked in acting like he was looking for a book."

"What'd you do?" Ron asked.

"What do you think? I blew up. I got in his face and demanded to know what he was doing there and who he was working for."

"Uh oh," Phil said.

"Not good," Ron said.

"Nope," Matt said.

Richard shook his head slowly.

"What?" Brian asked. "What would you guys have done?"

"He ran away, didn't he?" Ron asked.

"Well, yes, but..."

"And you don't know who he is." Ron said.

"You tipped your hand," Richard said. "You don't want to do that until you find out what you want to know."

"You sent him into hiding," Phil said.

Brian looked at his feet. Yes, but he wouldn't have done it differently. That kid needed to know he was found out. Of course, the guys were right. He'd lost his chance to find out more about the young man and who had sent him.

"I guess Karen questioned your reaction," Matt said.

"You could say that. I suppose she figured I'd blown a gasket. She'd never seen me angry before. That was a real awakening for a new bride so soon after the honeymoon. But, of course, the real problem was that I hadn't mentioned seeing him in Bruges."

"Told you," Matt said.

"Yeah. That was the worst part." Brian paused, thinking how the wives were probably discussing it at this very moment. "She was upset. We talked about it the rest of the day and night. I know it was stupid not to tell her when I saw the guy in Bruges."

"Can't argue with that," Phil said.

"She's convinced the stalker is related to her lawsuit. I suggested we pay the money and make the problem go away, but Karen wants to know the real reason she's being sued."

"You have to let her do what she needs to do," Matt said.

"Not just let her, but support her," Phil said.

"I know. I intend to. Richard, do you know of anything about the lawsuit that might shed light on this kid?"

"I can't talk about the case," Richard said.

"Oh," Brian said, feeling like he'd been slapped before he regained his composure. "You mean in front of the guys. I understand. We'll talk about it later."

"No. I mean I can't talk to you about it at all. Karen's my client. What she tells you is up to her, but I can't discuss it with you."

Brian grabbed a deep breath. "Oh, okay," he said. "I respect that. Maybe you could help, Ron. Do you know of any company problems that could be tied in with our stalker?"

"No. As far as I know, no one is threatening to sue again." Ron said. "If you want to find out who this kid is, you should talk to Liz."

"My Liz?"

"Yes. I walked in on her at the library when she was meeting with a group she called the Vengeance Squad. Introduced me to a computer science professor and a guy in a wheelchair. She didn't give me any details, but said they investigated crimes for people. Especially crimes the police have given up on solving. I bet they could find your stalker."

"Now that you mention it, she did borrow the bookmobile once to help apprehend some criminals in Galveston," Brian said. "But I wonder how they would know where to start looking."

"That's what they do," Ron said. "Want me to talk to her?"

"Sure." Knowing someone might help find that kid he ran off put Brian at ease for the first time since the incident.

"Shouldn't you talk to the police about this?" Richard asked.

"What would he report?" Phil asked. "Some guy comes in the bookmobile to check out a book and he gets run off because he looks like someone Brian saw in Europe. The cops aren't going to help. They might even arrest Brian."

Before Brian had a chance to agree with Phil, the wives showed up.

Karen walked directly to him and pecked his cheek. "You missed a fun movie," she said.

"Chick flick?"

"Of course."

"That's okay. I'm glad you liked it."

Karen kissed him. "I better go help with dinner."

As soon as Karen walked away, George came into the backyard and approached Brian.

"What's goin' on?" he asked.

"What do you mean?" Brian said.

"You still on your honeymoon mostly and you mopin' around like you lost your best friend."

Brian didn't know how Phil's father did it, but the man always seemed to read his mind. He stared at George, unsure of what to say. Should he tell how he'd not told Karen about seeing the photographer in Bruges? At least not told her soon enough to keep her from getting upset. Down deep he wanted more than anything to fully support Karen. So why did he feel his marriage was threatened by it? "I could use your help," he said. "Would you pray for me and Karen?"

"Of course. Do you want to tell me why?"

"I should, but I can't. Maybe later."

"I un'erstand. No need to tell me anythin', but just know you can. Meanwhile, I'm prayin'."

They walked together to join the rest of the guys at the smoker just as Phil took out the ribs. The aroma filled the area and they all sauntered over to the patio table, now filled a variety of side dishes and drinks.

CHAPTER ELEVEN

Three days after going to the movies with the Combine wives, Karen went to Cathy's house to visit her oldest and dearest friend. They'd met at church soon after Karen started teaching, and being about the same age and with the same deep Christian beliefs, it wasn't long before something clicked between them and they had been best friends ever since. They'd become Stephen Ministers together and both were active in the one-on-one, confidential Christian counseling program. Before Brian moved back to Austin, hardly a day went by when they didn't get together or at least talk on the phone.

She rang the doorbell and was surprised when Dudley opened the door.

"Come in." Cathy's husband appeared to have just gotten out of bed. His thinning hair hadn't seen a comb today and his drooping maroon and white striped pajamas were too large for him even though his ample-sized body would require an XXL.

"What are you doing home on a work day?" she asked.

"I'm sick," he said with a wink that meant he was playing hooky.

"You don't look sick," she said.

He feigned a cough, covering his mouth with one hand. "I'm not really sick." It was a whisper. "I just told them I was."

"I don't understand. You own your own furniture store. You can take off anytime you want to."

"I know. But I want my employees to think I only take off when I'm sick or on vacation. Just the way they do."

"Oh. So, why are you home?"

"No reason. I just decided to be sick today. I'm the boss, after all. Cathy is taking care of me." He smiled. "I like that best."

Karen had never understood Dudley. He was so helpless at home she wondered how he could possibly run a company. But she'd seen him at work. He was outgoing, personable, humorous at times, all the while exhibiting a professional air. At home, he was a destitute, often sloppy, child-like man who loved TV and relied on Cathy for all his needs. Karen had once asked her why she put up with it, and she explained that he put on such an act at work he was exhausted by the time he got home.

"Well, good for you," Karen said to Dudley. "Where is the lady of the house?"

"Sipping tea in the family room. Follow me."

Karen obeyed even though she'd been there hundreds of times.

"Good morning, Karen," Cathy said. "Dudley, when do you plan to go to work?"

"Not today," he said. "Can't." He offered his fake cough to let her know why.

"Well, if you're going to stay home, you need to get dressed and comb your hair. Now get out of here and leave us alone," she managed to say with love in her voice.

Dudley didn't seem offended by her remarks. He laughed and left the room.

"Tea?" Cathy asked as she poured Karen a cup. "No bookmobile run today, huh?"

"No. We have the day off because of maintenance."

"Good. You work too much for a retired person, anyway."

Karen wondered if she'd miss teaching after retiring last spring. So far it had been like any other summer, but soon she'd know what it would be like not to be at school.

They sipped tea in silence for a while. Karen enjoyed it, but she knew Cathy wouldn't wait long to quiz her.

"Tell me what's going on," Cathy said. "Not that you need a reason to come over. You look like you need to tell me something."

"I do. I want to tell you who came to visit us last week."

"Who? And why are you just now telling me?"

Karen knew Cathy would be peeved because Karen hadn't told her sooner. "He visited us in Germany and Belgium first. Then last Thursday he came waltzing into the bookmobile acting like anyone else. More than likely he was spying on us again."

"Who? Tell me."

Karen took a seat on the sofa and shifted her attention to her tea. She was about to say something that had been forming in her head, something she hadn't admitted to herself yet. "It was Ernest's son."

"Get out! Are you sure?"

"Well, no, but I know it in my gut."

"Tell me all the details." Cathy sat next to Karen and leaned in, waiting.

"A young man, about the right age to be Ernest's child, took photos of us sitting at an outdoor table in Hildesheim. I didn't think anything about it at the time, other than it was strange. I said something to Brian about wondering if the photographer had anything to do with the lawsuit, but I didn't seriously think he did. Not way over there in another country. The next thing I know the kid shows up on the bookmobile."

"Really? What'd you do?"

"Brian jumped him and scared him off. Frightened me some, too, to be honest."

"Brian or the young man?" Cathy asked.

"Brian. I'd never seen him so angry."

Cathy frowned. "Really? Did you find out what got him so riled?"

"Yes. It took some probing, but he finally told me he saw the kid in Bruges. He hadn't told me about it when it happened because he thought it might upset me."

"Wow. I bet that made it worse."

"It did. I know he meant well by keeping the information to himself in Bruges, but I let him know in no uncertain terms that I'd rather have known at the time what was going on. I told him I don't want him protecting my feelings."

"So, other than his age, what makes you think the young man is the offspring of your former husband?"

"While Brian was yelling at him, demanding that he tell who he worked for, the young man had the same look of fear I saw on Ernest's face when he learned he was dying. Not fear, exactly. More like acceptance."

"You saw a family resemblance."

"Yes. It was Ernest's son."

"Your stepson."

Karen hadn't thought about her relationship to the boy. Because of what Ernest had told her about his baby and the baby's mother, Karen never tried to make contact with either one after Ernest died. But, yes, he was her stepson.

"Did you tell Brian?"

"That the kid is my stepson? No, but I told him the young man had something to do with the lawsuit.

Brian thinks his ex-wife sent him to spy on us. I don't think so."

"Remember, you said you're not positive who he is."

"Reasonably sure."

"I guess we could find out," Cathy said, with a twinkle in her eye.

"What do you suggest?" They made a good investigative team when they'd worked together before, most recently investigating a high school athlete who had gotten a former student of Karen's pregnant.

"He knows you. But he doesn't know me. I could track him down through his mother. He might live with her. If not, he probably visits a lot. I could stake out her house and take a photo of him. That way you'll know for sure if he's the one."

"Good idea. Then we'll decide what to do next."

Karen finished her tea and stood. She sighed and sat again. "While I'm here I want to ask you a serious question."

Dudley walked in. He'd combed his hair and applied a liberal amount of hair oil. However, he hadn't gotten dressed.

"Dudley, dear, your hair looks nice, but didn't you forget something?"

He acted startled, tilted his head to the left, and stood there for a few seconds. "I don't think so."

"You were going to get out of those pajamas."

He grabbed his pajama top and snickered. "Oh, yeah. I forgot." He scooted out of the room.

"That man. I don't know what I'm going to do with him. If he ever gets Alzheimer's, how are we going to know? Now, tell me what's this serious question you have for me."

Karen cleared her throat. "Why is God punishing me?" She'd felt that way since the lawsuit papers were served, but this was the first time she'd said it out loud. "What did I do wrong for God to allow this lawsuit in my life? I've been faithful for so long. Do you think it's because of the miscarriage?"

Cathy went to her knees and took Karen's hands. "Listen to yourself," she said with her eyes fixed on Karen's. "You know better than that. You didn't do anything wrong. And even if you did, God forgives us for our sins. Unconditionally."

Karen bowed her head, knowing tears were falling down her cheeks. "I know. I should know that, but I've been feeling so alone in fighting this lawsuit."

Cathy tightened her grip on Karen's hands. "We need to pray about this."

Karen nodded, brushed away her tears, and bowed her head. The comfort of prayer yet to be spoken engulfed her and eased the stress she'd been carrying around since the wedding.

Cathy bowed and paused, continuing to hold Karen's hands. "Dear Lord," she said, "be close to Karen today and for as long as she's in pain. Remind her you are a loving, forgiving God. Remind her in particular of your love for her. Remind her how much you approve of all she does for others. Be with Brian. Make him strong and understanding.

"We are weak, dear Lord. When things go wrong in our lives, it's easy to think you've abandoned us even though you are always with us. We are never alone. Give us faith, strengthen that faith when doubts come to us, and remind us we are forgiven. Unconditionally forgiven."

Warmth washed over her and she knew God had surrounded her. Her mind and soul were once again in balance. She couldn't hold back the tears. "Thank you, Cathy. That was exactly what I needed."

Tears flowed from Cathy's eyes, too. Since that didn't happen often, it was more precious for Karen.

Suddenly a clear image popped into her head. "The shoebox!"

"What are you talking about?" Cathy stood.

Karen stood and paced. She rubbed her forehead trying to remember. "Ernest gave me an old shoebox containing his personal items. Junk, I called it at the time. You know, trinkets men save. Before he died, he asked me take care of it."

"A shoebox?"

"Yes. I've got to find that box. It must be important. At the end of your prayer, the memory of the box came to me so clearly I knew it was an answer to prayer."

"Why would that old shoebox be significant now?"

"I don't know. I remember looking through it at the time. There were some medals from the army, lapel pins, a few old coins. Also some letters and documents, but they didn't look important. A fancy certificate for completing a training session at work. Another for donating ten gallons of blood. The sort of official-looking cards and documents one hates to put in the trash, but for which there is little purpose, especially after death. I remember thinking at the time how sad that this was all that was left of the life of this wonderful, faithful man."

"Where is the shoebox?"

Karen brushed her hair back with her hands, straining her memory. "I don't know."

"Did you move it to Brian's house?"

"No. I would have remembered that. But I don't remember throwing it out, either. I wonder where it could be. I don't know why it's important, but I have to find it."

***

Karen hurried home, anxious to tell Brian about her visit with Cathy and the shoebox. He greeted her with a package from Harriet.

"Must be your phone," he said, kissing her on the cheek.

She unwrapped the package and found her phone and charger surrounded with bubble wrap, along with a money order. There was a handwritten note in the bottom of the box. "Here's a note from Harriet," she said.

"Read it. I'd love to hear how she's doing."

"I'll never forget the love and friendship you gave me when I was stranded and all alone in Bruges. I cringe when I think what could have happened to me if you hadn't noticed I needed help. Thanks for the use of your phone, and don't forget to listen to that mean phone message. I thank God for you and Brian every day. Harriet."

"She's a nice lady," Karen said as she turned on the phone. "I guess we better check this message." She pressed the voice mail icon.

"Yeah. I wonder who it could be from," he said.

She pressed the speaker button so Brian could hear, too.

The voice was male and gruff. "Listen carefully. No way you gonna win that lawsuit. Make a decent offer and it'll all be over. But hurry. This deal ain't gonna last forever."

Karen turned to Brian.

"Now," he said, "we have a reason to call the police."

"You're right."

She called Richard at home and told him about it. "Should we call the police?"

"Bring it to the office tomorrow. Let me listen and we'll decide on the best approach. But, yes, I think we will probably want to notify law enforcement. Let's do it from my office."

"What time's best," she asked.

"How's noon sound? I'm pretty booked up, but I always save time for lunch."

"I'll be there with two Thundercloud subs and you furnish the drinks."

He quickly answered. "Deal."

She didn't get around to telling Brian about Cathy's prayer and the shoebox until the next morning.

CHAPTER TWELVE

Karen stopped at Thundercloud Subs on West 12th Street thirty minutes before her meeting with Richard. She ordered her favorite, avocado on wheat and selected the California club for him. As she waited for her food she thought about her discussion with Brian at breakfast. That's when she'd told him about her meeting with Cathy and how her best friend's prayer had triggered Karen's memory of the shoebox Ernest had left with her. Brian wasn't as excited about the news as Karen was, and he didn't seem to appreciate the significance of the revelation. Perhaps if she could explain why the shoebox was important to the case, he'd understand. But, she didn't know. Not yet, anyway.

He'd offered to come with her to meet with Richard, and he'd conceded that due to the phone message, the unusual events they'd experienced were probably related to the lawsuit. That was a huge admission for him and she appreciated it. Then why did she discourage him from coming with her today by telling him how important it was to take the bookmobile out on its usual route? She knew why. The lawsuit was hers and she wanted to make the decisions herself without Brian's influence. Even though he said he supported her totally, and she knew deep down he loved her, there was still something that made her think he'd settle in an instant if it was left to him.

When she got to Richard's office perspiration formed on her upper lip and she breathed faster than usual. This ridiculous lawsuit ate away at her mainly because she didn't understand it and couldn't fix it. Her life had been happy and free of conflict after her divorce from Steve. For some unknown reason, God wanted her to think about that time with Ernest and face it head on. He didn't seem to care how this lawsuit affected her marriage to Brian by consuming her days and nights.

Richard met her in the lobby and they went to the conference room to eat and talk. She placed the sandwiches and chips on the long mahogany table and took a seat in front of the avocado one.

"I have soft drinks and coffee," Richard said. "Which one do you prefer?"

"Do you have Dr Pepper?"

"Sure." He left the room and returned shortly with two cans of Dr Pepper and two paper cups.

After they finished eating, Karen played the voicemail for Richard. He asked her to repeat it several times.

"You don't recognize the voice, do you?" he asked.

"No." She paused as she considered his question. "Maybe. I'm not sure. Did you notice the English accent? It's subtle, perhaps feigned. That voice reminds of someone. I just can't think who it is."

"Well, if it comes to you, let me know right away. I don't think we can say there is a criminal threat issued here by the caller. Still, I want to get it in the official records in case you get more calls. I'll file a complaint with the police, but I'm sure there's nothing they can do. Since the caller refers to the lawsuit against you and is attempting to influence what you do in the case, there's a definite threat. That is, if you don't settle now, things will get worse. I doubt if the caller is directly related to the case, but, with your permission, I'll let the plaintiff's attorney listen to it and see if he can identify the person."

"Do you think Cloris's lawyer would tell us if he knows who the caller is?"

"I'm not sure. But I do know he'll want to distance himself from actions such as this if at all possible. I'll transcribe the message and file a complaint with the court just in case."

"Okay," Karen said. "You have my permission to do whatever you want to with the phone message."

"Thanks. I'll call him this afternoon. I talked to him yesterday, but it was before you called."

"What did he have to say?"

Richard smiled and shook his head. "I'm beginning to learn more about what's going on. Texas laws for child support are strictly enforced and they're taking advantage of that."

"I know you told me before, but I still don't understand how they could sue me for child support. Besides the fact that he's not my son, he's not a child. And, to top it off, there is no record of my being liable for child support."

Richard nodded. "The fact that he's not a child doesn't matter. Remember, Brian asked about that last time. The statute of limitations for collecting unpaid child support is four years after the child reaches eighteen. Heath Brower, your stepson, turned twenty-two one week after they filed the case."

In all the years since Ernest's death, Karen had never once thought of Heath as her stepson. Cathy had mentioned it and now Richard did, too. The concept made her dizzy.

"But why me? I wasn't responsible for supporting him. I was married to his father for a brief time. That's all. When Ernest died, I'm sure Heath received social security benefits. I remember providing a death certificate to some lawyer Cloris sent over. What else do they want?"

"Social Security survivor benefits don't erase the obligation to pay child support. They have a court order showing the amount Ernest agreed to pay. On top of that they added interest for twenty-two years, bringing the demanded amount up to close to two million dollars. I didn't do the math but, even if the calculations are off, it'll be a substantial amount."

"I understand that. But they don't have a court order saying I'm responsible for the boy."

"No. Their claim is that you received property from Ernest that should have gone to support Heath."

Karen took a drink of her Dr Pepper and wondered why she felt light-headed. "I never talked to Ernest about child support payments. I remember when he gave up trying to see the boy because he couldn't afford legal representation and he didn't want to impose on me more. I offered to pay for an attorney, but he wouldn't accept more from me. He'd been a successful business man at one time, but he had lost many of his assets in a divorce from his first wife. He lost some in bad business deals, and some disappeared during the economic downfall. When he learned the cancer was terminal, he changed. It was as if he didn't care about anything. He quit working. Didn't go out. That was about the same time Cloris started harassing him about the child support payments. From then on he lost all desire to live."

"Did he give you any of his assets when you two were married, as they claim?"

"That was a long time ago. I'll have to see if I have any records from that time. But yes, he gave me a vacant lot he owned. It was the only asset he had left when we married. I thought he owned a house, too, but it turned out it'd gone back to the bank. He gave the vacant lot to me to help pay expenses while he lived with me. I had good medical insurance, so that wasn't a consideration. I told him he didn't have to, but he wanted to repay me for room and board. It was a matter of pride with him. He had no income and no money by that time and the lot was all he had left."

"What happened to the property?"

"After he died, I tried to sell it, but the only offer I got was less than a thousand dollars so I decided to hold on to it until the economy improved."

"Do you still own the property?"

"No. I held on to it for about four years and sold it when Julie was born to start a college fund."

"How much did you get for it?"

"By that time property values had risen and it brought in about two thousand dollars, hardly enough for one year at the University of Texas. But Steve and I added to the fund over the years and, by the time Julie graduated from high school, the fund had grown to a sum large enough to pay her way for four years."

"Why did you do it?"

The question shook her. "Do what?"

"Marry Ernest."

Karen walked from the chair to the window and looked out. Her answer came to her with ease. "Ernest was well respected at our church. Everyone knew him and cared for him. When I was new there and just starting out in my teaching career, he helped me. When I applied for my teaching job he offered to be a character reference for me. I think he also talked to someone at administration about me. He gave me a part-time job at his office to help pay off my student loans and let me work after school and weekends. I heard rumors about how he helped many people in the church in a variety ways. He made one mistake that I know of and it ruined his life."

"What mistake was that?"

"He got someone pregnant."

"Cloris Parker."

"Yes."

"I know about your premarital pregnancy and how it affected you. I know you never told anyone about it and the miscarriage until many years later. Is it fair to say you wished you'd had someone to help you at the time and that made you more aware of what Ernest faced with his son?"

Karen sat at the table across from Richard. "Perhaps. But my situation was different. I had a miscarriage and didn't have a child. Ernest had a son with a woman he didn't love. She forced him to marry her by going to our pastor. After the baby was born, she fought him every time he tried to see him. I was more concerned with the fact Ernest was dying alone. When Ernest got sick, and knew he didn't have much time left, he no longer cared about any of it. A son he'd tried hard to see suddenly became unimportant. I watched him die months before he passed away, if you know what I mean."

Unwanted tears raced down her face.

"Did you love him?" Richard asked.

Karen wiped away the tears with the back of her hand. "It was a strange relationship. I think I was in love with the man he used to be. I disliked the man he'd become. When he died, I tried to forget it happened instead of mourning his death. That's why talking about it is hard now. I can't continue to push those memories away if someone keeps bringing them back. I've got to face them with what I now know. I've studied grieving and dying since then and I claim to trust God completely. I must confess that having to relive this unpleasant time in my life has been difficult."

Richard nodded and seemed to be in deep thought. "I've got to be honest with you. If you look at this case in a strictly financial way, you'll be better off to settle with them and not go to court. Based on the value of the lot Ernest gave you, we could give them ten or twenty thousand and they'd be glad to get it."

The thought of settling forced her to catch her breath. That was what Brian wanted. Her hands trembled slightly. "No. Ernest wanted me to have that lot. I want to go to court if that's what it takes."

"Even if it's costly?"

"Yes."

"I understand." Richard picked up a folder and opened it. "Here's something to consider. Since we talked last, I've learned that the attorney for the plaintiff is Cloris's brother. Hank Unger. He's a second career lawyer who is probably looking for experience and probably isn't charging Cloris much, if anything."

"Do you think that's why she filed the lawsuit? To provide experience for her brother?"

Richard shook his head. "No. I'm not saying that. And, remember, this is mostly conjecture on my part. We may never learn what's in her heart." He put the folder down on the table and glanced into her eyes. "I think Cloris or someone close to her read about your pending marriage to Brian and figured there might be a way to profit from your past connection to Heath."

"That's what Brian said." How could anyone do that?

"It happens more than you might think," Richard said.

She hoped there was more to the case than greedy people trying to take Brian's money. "I keep looking for something more important than money. I'd like to think God put me in this situation for a reason. A significant reason."

"I hope you're right." Richard paused so long Karen began to wonder if the meeting was over, but then he continued. "Hank asked me to put together a settlement offer. Since we must respond, I suggest we write them and say it's not proper to make a settlement offer since you are not liable for your ex-husband's unpaid child support."

"That sounds good," Karen said.

"In the meantime, find any financial records you have from that period of time and bring them in. Income tax returns, title transfers, anything you think could be related."

"Okay. I haven't moved all my old files yet. They're at my house in Sunset Valley. I wanted to go through and throw out unneeded junk before moving what's left to Brian's place."

"Okay. Call me when you're ready and we'll schedule another meeting." Richard stood. "I'll contact Hank and let him know about the phone message and tell him we won't settle."

Karen stood. It would've been easy to tell Richard to pay them what they wanted and resolve the case. But something wouldn't let her do it. "From the beginning I've believed this is a God thing. I believe I've been put in this position of defending myself for a reason. If all I do is settle and give them money, I'll never know what God had in mind."

"I can't help you there, but I'll do whatever you wish. I'm just warning you that no matter what happens it will be costly. Even if you win, you lose."

"I understand, and I appreciate what you're saying." She bowed her head and paused quietly before looking into his face. "I pray for guidance every day. For myself and for everyone else involved in the case. Today, I want to fight the accusations all the way. If I'm led otherwise, I'll let you know."

"So, God is the lead attorney in this case."

Karen smiled. "Yes. You might say that."

At the door, she turned back. "Richard, do you think you could get me a recent photo of Heath?"

"Hmm. I don't know. I'll try."

"Thanks." Cathy would be disappointed if it was that easy, but Karen wanted to see for herself if Heath was the one who was stalking her.

When she got to her car, someone had left her another message. This time in broad daylight on Congress Avenue two blocks from the Capitol grounds. A message that didn't make sense. All four tires on her car were flat.

She called road service, and waited until help arrived.

Dear Lord, don't forget you promised not to give me more than I can handle. Just wanted you to know, I'm reaching a breaking point here. Okay?

CHAPTER THIRTEEN

After road service replaced the valves and aired up her tires, Karen was on her way. Her spirit was as deflated as her tires had been. She didn't know if the incident was related to the lawsuit or just a juvenile prank. She felt out of control as if the whole world was against her. She needed to talk to someone. She usually turned to Cathy at times like this, but not today. Cathy would just say to get over it. And she'd be right. But Karen wanted to talk to someone who would listen, someone who didn't know her like Cathy did. Kay popped into her head. Since Brian moved to Austin and Karen and Kay had gotten back together, there was a special closeness between them, the type she didn't have with Cathy.

By the time Karen had decided to talk to Kay, she realized she was headed toward the McCullough house. But when she got there, Kay wasn't home. Only George.

"Come on in," he said. "Kay'll be home soon, I 'spect."

Karen remembered the time Brian told her how much George had helped him when he was discouraged. Could it be that today it was George she needed to talk to? Perhaps.

"Thank you," she said as she went in, trusting God to lead her to the right person.

"Come and sit." George motioned toward the sofa. He straightened his bowtie and sat at the other end. "I heard all about that terrible lawsuit of yours. It must be hard havin' to rehash that painful time in your life."

"Yes it is," Karen said. "That's the reason I wanted to talk to Kay. The case is so discouraging. I don't understand why God wants me to go through this. It's as if I'm being punished for some reason."

"Now, Miss Karen, you know better. God's not punishin' you."

George reached over to the lamp table next to the sofa and picked up a black leather-bound Bible. The edges of the book flared open from years of use leaving the spine half the thickness of the page edges. Before reading, he adjusted wire-framed glasses with the small round lenses he hardly ever peered through.

"Remember in Acts 9 where God asks Ananias to go put his hands on Saul?"

Karen smiled. "I'm not a Bible scholar like you. Tell me about it."

"Well, you're like Ananias. You're a good Christian, but you've been called to get into this lawsuit for some reason. The results can be devastatin', but they can also be won'erful. We mere humans can't know until God reveals the intention to us. We have to be open to what God is callin' us to do. And, remember, it may not seem like it sometimes, but eventually, good overcomes evil. Ananias was asked to step outside his comfort zone. And it sounds to me like you're uncomfortable."

Karen couldn't believe how accurately George explained it. "You're right," she said. "I'm definitely outside my comfort zone. But that doesn't explain why God has asked me to do this."

"I'd say it's because you're special." George said with a grin.

"How's that?"

"You've been called by God for some purpose. That doesn't happen to ever'body."

"So, I should be pleased about the lawsuit." Her body relaxed for the first time since leaving the law office. "Thank you, George."

"You're welcome." He flipped the pages of his Bible as he lifted it in the air. "Now I'm not sure if this will help you with your particular situation, but in Romans 12:8 it says if you have the gift of encouragement then you should devote yourself to it. I have observed you this past year and if anyone has that gift it's you. You're an encouragin' woman, Miss Karen."

"I am?" She had a talent for helping others, but she hadn't thought of that talent as the gift of encouragement mentioned in the Bible.

"You certainly are. Now I know you and Brian are disagreein' about how to handle this court case. I hear things around here you know. He wants to settle and you don't."

"That's right," she said.

"What you need to look at is why you two are disagreein'."

"That's simple. I want to know the reason I'm being sued and he wants to do whatever he can to get it over with."

"I believe you want to learn why they're suin' you because of your gift of encouragement. You want to fight the case to help the ones suin'. Not just yourself. Now, Brian doesn't think about them. He only thinks of you and he feels gettin' the case over with would be best for you."

What George said made sense. She had to suffer through the lawsuit to help Cloris or Heath. Or both. She hoped doing so wouldn't affect her marriage.

***

Karen went from Kay and Phil's house to her Sunset Valley home. She wanted to look for the shoebox Ernest had left with her and gather any financial papers she had from that period of time. She still didn't know where to look for the trinkets Ernest left so she started searching for the papers Richard wanted first.

She was sitting at the desk in her home office digging through the file drawer when her cell phone rang. It was Brian.

She should have called him to let him know when she'd be home. And she hadn't told him about the latest fiasco; the flat tires. Nor was she ready to tell him she suspected their stalker was her stepson. "Hello." She leaned back in her chair.

"Where are you?" he asked before she had a chance to say more. "I thought you'd be home before me. Are you still at the law office?"

"No. I'm sorry. I should have called you earlier. I got delayed at Richard's office and then I went to talk to Kay."

"Why were you delayed? Is everything okay?"

"Nothing serious. When I left the law office, all four tires on my car were flat. I called road service and all they did was replace the valves and air up the tires. I was out of there in less than an hour. Luckily, the tires weren't slashed. It just gripes me that someone would do that."

"Do you think it has something to do with the lawsuit?" Brian asked.

"Yes, but it seems so juvenile."

"Could be what they consider a warning. Be careful. They may start to escalate the vandalism."

"I'll watch out for anything suspicious. I'm over at my house right now trying to find some financial documents Richard asked for, but I'll be leaving soon."

"Financial documents?"

"Yes. Cloris is claiming that property I received from Ernest should have gone to pay child support. Evidently, that's the basis for the lawsuit."

"Is it true?"

"Ernest deeded a vacant lot to me to help pay his expenses while he lived with me. I'll tell you more about it when I get home."

"Okay. When? And do we have plans for dinner?"

She had spent the whole afternoon thinking about the lawsuit and hadn't thought of eating. "You want to eat out tonight? I should be through here in less than an hour."

"Sure. Sounds good. I'll see you when you get here."

She found the files she was looking for and pulled them out. Just as she stood to leave the room a shadow passed by the curtained window. Her heartbeat went up quickly and she froze.

Several deep breaths later, she regained her composure. With the files in hand, she walked quietly to the living room where she could see out the large window. No one was there. She'd left her car out front instead of in the garage since she hadn't planned to be there long. She had wanted to search for the shoebox, but decided to save that for another day. She waited a few more minutes. Since no one appeared, she made a run for it and reached her car without incident. *Help me, Lord. It's getting scary out here.*

***

The Austin History Center was on the corner of Guadalupe and Ninth Streets, facing north. The massive cream-colored limestone building matched the Travis County Courthouse a block away. Wooldridge Park separated the two buildings. The bowl-shaped park with a gazebo in the center didn't obstruct the view from the History Center to the County Courthouse because of the depth of the basin.

Brian had visited the History Center many times, but he'd always entered through the back door where they loaded the bookmobile. For his meeting with Liz today, he parked on Ninth Street and walked toward the main entrance. For the first time he saw the plaque that said the building had been the Austin Public Library from 1933 to 1979, and stopped to read.

"The Italian Renaissance Style features work of some of Austin's finest craftsmen, including ironworker Fortunant Wiegle, wood-carver Peter Mansbendel and fresco artist Harold 'Bubi' Jessen."

Interesting. He might come back and look up those names someday. As he walked down the main hallway looking for the O'Henry Room, Brian ignored that slight twinge of guilt he felt because he hadn't told Karen about the meeting with Liz. If only he hadn't run off the kid when he had him trapped on the bookmobile. The guy could be dangerous. He was probably the one who let all the air out of Karen's tires. Brian had to find him and stop him, but he didn't have enough evidence to take the issue to the police. He needed advice first, and perhaps Liz and her friends could help.

He found the room at the end of the hall. The walls were covered with mahogany shelves filled with books.

Liz and two men sat at one of the four tables. As soon as he saw her, he readied himself for her trademark bear hug.

"Come in, Brian!" After the hug, she said, "Meet my friends."

One of the men stood to greet Brian. The other was in a wheelchair. The one standing appeared to be in his mid-thirties. He wore a dark blue polo shirt and khaki slacks. His blond hair and beard were both closely trimmed.

"Hi, I'm Chris. Nice to meet you," he said.

The man in the wheelchair rolled closer to Brian. "Call me Tex," he said, holding out his hand.

Liz smiled. "Let's sit and talk about what we can do for you."

Liz sat at the end of the table while Chris took the chair across from Brian. He took out a pad of paper which he placed on the table in front of him along with a pen. Brian watched him go through several motions lining up the pad and the pen. Tex had a laptop open and ready. A ten-gallon cowboy hat sat on the end of the table near him. He seemed to have a constant smile on his face while Chris appeared to be more serious.

Liz cleared her throat and all turned their eyes toward her. "I wanted to start by giving Brian a brief description of what we can do to help." She nodded toward Chris. "Dr. McCowan is a computer science professor at Austin Community College. Naturally, his expertise is the use of computers for investigations. He teaches a class on digital forensics, but he knows more about cyberspace than anyone I know."

Chris nodded and straightened the perfectly aligned note pad and pen in front of him.

"Tex works part-time here at the library and has for several years. He took all of Chris's computer science classes at ACC, but now he goes to the University of Texas on a special scholarship." Liz nodded slightly toward Brian when she mentioned the scholarship. Brian suspected Tex was the recipient of one he and Phil provided. He remembered talking to Liz about someone she felt deserved the help.

Liz turned her attention to Brian. "Why don't you tell us what's happened and why you need us?"

"I'd like you to find someone for me," Brian said. "A young man is following my wife or me. He showed up in Germany and Belgium. After we got back to Austin, he came aboard the bookmobile. That's when I asked him what he was doing and scared him off. I suspect he's still following us, but I can't be sure. He's probably being more careful about it since we tipped our hand. The other day someone let all the air out of my wife's tires. All four tires. I don't know if the kid did it or not, but I think so."

"What does he look like?" Liz asked.

"Early twenties, maybe. About six-three, chunky, but not fat. Every time we saw him he wore a white tee shirt and blue jeans with a cowboy belt. In Europe he wore an English driving cap, but he didn't have it on when he came on the bookmobile."

Liz turned to Brian. "Do you have any idea who might want to follow you or Karen?"

"Karen's ex-husband's wife and son sued Karen recently, so naturally my wife thinks the stalker has something to do with the lawsuit." He pushed a file folder toward Liz. "This folder contains all I know about the case and the people involved, but there's not much to go on."

Liz took the folder and didn't open it. "I see you have two additional folders with you. Does that mean there are other suspects?"

Brian picked up the next folder. "Yes. This one contains information about my ex-wife, Judy. She has threatened to sue me on a number of occasions and I wouldn't put it past her to hire someone as incompetent as the guy who's been following us to try to get more alimony." He pushed the folder to Liz.

"And the other?" Liz nodded to the remaining folder.

"This one contains information about my company and the previous owners."

"What kind of company do you have?" Chris asked.

"It's an unusual mix of products and services. I started out thirty-plus years ago in Redondo Beach, California, doing anything related to computers. The industry grew fast and I managed to get in on the ground floor with a number of products. We're the exclusive distributor for several computer-aided manufacturing machines as well as the provider of custom software and hardware."

"Is there a problem with the company?" Tex asked. "Why would someone go after you?"

"I retired a few years ago and sold the company to a group of investors who nearly bankrupted it. Along with a few other stock holders I regained control of the company and it's once again successful. The group that messed it up are out and not happy about it. I think they might be behind the stalking."

Liz held up the three folders. "Well, looks like we have what we need to find out."

"All you want to know for now is who the young man is and who he works for, right?" Chris asked.

"Yes," Brian said.

"Do you want us to rough him up?" Tex asked.

"Tex!" Liz said. "Don't be silly. Brian doesn't know you're joking."

"Who's joking," Tex said.

CHAPTER FOURTEEN

A month passed with little progress in the court case. She didn't want to settle, but she wanted the lawsuit over with. She wanted her life back, her life as Mrs. Donelson, the life that had just begun. Richard had followed her instructions and turned down the plaintiff's request for a settlement offer. After that, it seemed to Karen like the only activity in the case was a battle of words. Papers flew from one office to the other, sometimes several in one day. She received copies of everything and little of it made sense. She had yet to see a picture of Heath to prove he'd followed them to Europe. She also had not remembered where she'd put the shoebox Ernest gave her.

Brian hadn't mentioned it lately, but she knew he wanted to pay off Cloris and Heath no matter what the cost. Karen continued to believe God wanted her to fight the lawsuit.

"Well, how did it go today?" Brian asked when she got home.

She'd spent the day at the courthouse answering questions.

"I hated it," she said.

"Why?"

"How would you like spending the day answering questions about a time in your life you want to forget?"

"Well, why did you?" Brian asked.

"I had to. It's the law. Each party gets to asks questions. Today was my day to answer. It's called a deposition."

"Did you know ahead of time what to expect?"

"Yes. Richard gave me a list of questions a week ago so that I could prepare. But then they have some freedom in expanding into more detail if they feel it's needed."

"Why didn't you write down your answers and give that to them?"

"I don't know. I think it has to be done in court and under oath. I do get to see the transcript and make changes if something recorded is not correct."

"Deposition in court and transcriptions. I guess Richard had to be there all day, too. Boy, this is going to be expensive, isn't it?"

"It is. Does that bother you?"

"No, just saying."

She wished he understood why she wanted to fight the case.

"Did you get to quiz Cloris and Heath?" he asked.

"No, not yet. I prepared questions for Richard to ask when we get our turn, though." She was anxious to hear what they had to say and learn more about why the suit was filed against her. Was the goal to cause her financial loss? To interfere with her happiness? It was difficult to come up with relevant questions when she didn't know too much about the situation. She wished she could sit down and talk to them face to face without having to do it in court.

"Were they there today when you got deposed?"

"She was, but not Heath. She looked bad. She whispered to her brother constantly as he asked me questions. During a break, when I walked near her, I smelled alcohol."

"Really?" Brian shook his head.

"Cathy said she noticed it, too."

"Oh, I didn't know Cathy was there," Brian said.

"Yes. I guess it makes sense. She knew Ernest and Cloris before she met me."

"How'd she do on the stand?"

"Good. She added information I didn't know."

"I hope they subpoena me. I've got a few things I'd like to tell them."

***

The following Monday, the bookmobile was parked at a retirement home in northeast Austin. Karen and

Brian were alone, but they wouldn't be for long. The social director there usually brought in a group of residents about this time. Today, Brian sat at the front desk so Karen could use the computer on the desk in the rear.

"Oh, piffle," she said, looking up from the computer screen. "I just got an e-mail from Marie."

"Who's Marie?"

"Richard's assistant. It seems Cloris's attorney is pulling another stalling tactic."

"He's good at that," Brian said.

"Yes. I'd love to hear what Cloris and Heath have to say while sworn to tell the truth. Apparently, Cloris doesn't want to be deposed. I think she doesn't want Heath to be put on the stand. No matter how bad she is, she's a mother and I bet she doesn't want her son to know what she did twenty-two years ago.

"Listen to this."

Privileged and Confidential

Karen:

With regard to your question about Cloris and Heath's depositions, we have been asking for dates to do so, but have not heard a word from them. I guess we could force the issue by asking the court to schedule them to be deposed, but that might get them fired up and cause them to do more delaying tactics. If you would like for us to push this more, please let me know the dates you are available during the last week of the month and I will get their deposition scheduled.

Marie.

"I told her to go ahead and force the issue. I guess they did. Here's a follow-up e-mail I just got from Richard."

I am sorry I have not responded sooner. For some reason I thought that we had communicated to you that no news was really good news, at least in my estimation.

I expect this case to get heated up next month, because I finally ran into the opposing attorney who said that he wanted to finish your deposition and Cathy's also, (he thinks they are entitled to more time from you two, but we'll fight that) and I told him I needed to make arrangements for Heath's deposition.

I've decided to file what is called a motion for summary judgment to get Cloris out of the case entirely. This will cause her some problems because, like you suspected, her brother said she wants to protect her son from knowing what happened back then.

I'll try to call you when I am back in town next week about scheduling, etc.

Richard Davis

"So, not only are they not being deposed yet, they're trying to get more time to quiz me and Cathy. I've told them everything I know. Cathy has, too."

Brian didn't want to say it again because it would irritate her, but he wished she would settle. Before he could comment, a gang of senior citizens poured in asking all sorts of questions. One wanted a book on genealogy and another inquired about the latest Grisham book.

***

A week later, Brian loaded the bookmobile for their daily run while Karen went around the corner from the loading dock to fetch two coffees to go.

"Well, you just missed the fun," he said when she returned. "I'm being sued by Cloris, too. The process server just left." Brian grabbed a box of books ready to carry into the bookmobile.

"You ready to pay her off yet?" As soon as the words were out of his mouth he regretted it.

"No."

"I'm sorry. I meant it to be a joke and then I realized how it would hurt you. That's the last thing I want to do."

"I'm sorry you were sued, but you know how I feel about settling." Her words were clipped.

"I know and I'm truly sorry for bringing it up again. The process server asked for you, too. Just for fun, I told him you'd quit working here and left town. He probably knew I lied, but if he tells the client, maybe it'll shake her up."

"I hate this," she said. "As soon as I get used to what's going on, they change it up. I like to have some control over my life. Not knowing what's going on throws me off balance."

"Me too."

***

It didn't take long for Karen to get her papers. The process server met them at the first stop. He nodded at Brian with a smile as he handed Karen the document.

She read it over, but it made no sense. She called Richard and, with the phone in speaker mode, read the document to him.

"I can't believe what they're doing," Richard said. "They know I represent you and they know to file all papers with me. What's happening is that they've filed a new case and are assuming I'm the attorney for the first case only. Don't worry, I'll take care of it."

"Does that mean the old case is dropped?" Karen asked.

"No. At least I haven't received anything about it yet," Richard said.

"Oh," Karen said, "I forgot to mention Brian was served, too."

"He was? Well, we'll see about that. I'll file a Rule 13 right away."

"Rule 13?"

"Yes. That authorizes the imposition of sanctions against an attorney who files a pleading that is groundless or in bad faith. Including Brian in the case is clearly groundless."

"So he doesn't need to do anything? He's listening in here, by the way."

"Well, I'll need to see what is in his papers, but I'm sure we can take care of it."

Brian leaned toward the phone. "I'll bring the document to your office today. Listen, I heard what you said about them filing a new case. I thought the statute of limitations would prevent that."

"It would seem like it since they just filed the first case in time. But, from what I heard, they've attached it to the first case to make it legal."

They all said good bye and Karen disconnected the call.

"Sometimes I wish I could do what you want and settle the case. You know, get it over with so we can enjoy our life together more. I know you didn't bargain for this when you married me. But I think I should stay with the case, keep fighting it, because of Heath."

"Why?"

"Well, in a sense, he's family."

"Family? Heath?"

"He's as much family to me as Amy is."

"Amy? That's different. You're my wife. Of course my daughter would be family."

Karen had prayed about what to do. Brian didn't want to hear about Heath being family, but what did God want? She was careful to include Cloris and Heath in her prayers, plus their lawyer. With Brian getting defensive about Heath, she decided not to mention she'd talked to Cathy and Richard about getting a photo of Heath to see if he was the one following them around the world.

"Does Richard think Cloris has a case?"

"No. He thinks we'll win if it goes to court. But they've managed to block Richard's attempts to have the case thrown out. The judge is approving the depositions and keeping the case going, without studying the details, apparently thinking the plaintiff will provide more proof as time goes by. Richard thinks they might be trying to force me to pay legal fees while giving Cloris's brother courtroom experience. She doesn't have to pay a cent for legal expenses since her brother doesn't need the money. He's probably paying the court costs as well. Richard has filed a petition requesting details about Cloris's legal fees, but her lawyer hasn't responded yet."

"That's terrible."

"Yeah. Richard agrees with you about how to approach the case. He said I'd come out ahead financially by settling. He said his cost could get into the six figures, and that's with the family discount."

"Family discount." Brian laughed. "Combine discount, he means. So, what are you going to do?"

He waited for a response. Even so, she paused as long as she could. What she had to say was difficult for her.

"I've prayed about this every day since the wedding. I'm at peace with it now, but it's hard to explain. I tried to tell Richard, but all he hears is that I want to fight back. I think something good will come out of this. God has a reason for me to be in a lawsuit and if I throw money at it, your money, I may never know what God wanted. Does that make sense?"

Brian's eyes narrowed and he froze for a few seconds before he slowly nodded his head. "Yes. I understand. You say 'my money,' but you know everything I have is yours."

"I know," Karen said. "I'm not used to the money part yet. I was on a tight budget for many years and haven't learned to think the way you do. I remember last year when you were sued and your bank accounts were frozen. You hadn't had to worry about money for so long you didn't know what to do. Do you recall?"

He smiled as he shook his head. "Yes. I'll never forget. I don't want that to happen again. But you have to admit, I don't waste money."

"Oh, I'm not saying you do. It's just that you have always had enough to do what you wanted to do. I know you donate a lot to different causes and you especially like to help disadvantaged people. I know you put Phil through medical school."

"How did you know that?"

"He told me."

"Yeah, he was just guessing. It was an anonymous donor."

She smiled. "I understand. Getting back to Richard...I also told him I'd keep praying about what to do."

She thought about the shoebox. It seemed to pop into her head every day now. If only she could find it.

***

Two days later Brian steered the bookmobile into their usual parking spot at the Allandale strip mall. He set the parking brake before climbing out. Karen opened the door on the passenger side and set out the step for patrons to enter more easily. He opened the back door climbed up the steps and stole a quick kiss before anyone showed up. She kissed him back with a smile that made him remember why he loved her so.

She turned her chair around to face the library and he started the generator for the air conditioner before going to the checkout station at the rear of the vehicle. His cell phone rang as he sat down.

"Brian, it's Ron. How'd your meeting with Liz go?"

Brian hadn't told Karen about that meeting, but there was no reason why he shouldn't. He waved to Karen, motioned with his head toward the door. "It's Ron. I'll take it outside."

She nodded and he went out the back door in time to see a woman, fifty or so, in a brown skirt and bright yellow blouse, entering the front door. He didn't recognize her as one of the regulars, but she looked like dozens of other women from the neighborhood.

"The meeting was good," he said to Ron. "I think the guys will be able to find out what I need to know."

"Okay. Just wanted to make sure."

"Thanks, Ron."

Brian pressed the end button and put the phone in his pocket. As he walked toward the bookmobile, he heard a muffled scream. It sounded like Karen, but he wasn't sure. He jumped into the bookmobile through the back door. What he saw made him freeze.

Karen sat in the librarian chair facing the rear of the bookmobile. The woman he'd seen enter through the front door stood behind her with a handful of Karen's hair in one hand and a large kitchen knife in the other. The knife reflected light in all directions as the woman twisted it around close to Karen's throat. Karen's eyes told Brian not to move.

"Hold it right there, mister, or this woman gets it." The assailant's voice was strong and sure even though her actions were less than steady.

Seeing her from this vantage point, Brian realized she didn't look as much like the other patrons as he'd thought. Her hair could use a combing and her clothes were rumpled.

Brian held up the palms of his hands to let her know he wasn't a threat. "Okay. What do you want? I've got some money here I can give you. Just put your knife down and we'll give you whatever you want," he said as calmly as possible.

"Just git. That's what you can do for me. Git."

"Okay. We'll leave as soon as you put the knife down," Brian said.

The woman jerked Karen's hair, forcing her head back further. Her eyes were wide open now, the blade pressed flat against her throat.

"Humf. You think I'm stupid. If I put this down, you'll grab me."

"Well, how can we leave if you don't let her go?" Brian asked.

"I want you to go, not her. God told me to drive this machine and that's what I'm going to do." She motioned toward the driver's seat.

"God wouldn't want you to drive drunk, would he?" Karen asked.

"Oh," the woman said, followed by a giggle. "You're right. Not good to drive after you've had a little drinky poo. I guess you'll have to drive."

As the woman attempted to move Karen to the driver's seat, Brian waited for an opportunity to rush her and take the knife, but he didn't see a safe opening. Drunk or not, the knife was close to Karen's throat and he didn't want to take a chance on what the crazy lady might do.

"Wait," Brian said. "I'm the driver. She's never driven this vehicle before." This was a lie, but the woman wouldn't know.

The woman acted startled by that, but not for long. "Not you. Her. I don't like you. I'm sure she can drive this thing. You go out the back door right now if you don't want me to use this knife on this pretty lady."

"I'm not leaving until you let her go," Brian said.

"It's okay," Karen said. He didn't want to leave, but she pleaded with her eyes for him to do so.

"Are you sure?" He ignored the woman and talked to Karen.

"Yes. I think I can drive."

"Okay," he said to the woman. "But you won't get away with this." He could call for help as soon as he got outside, but that wouldn't help Karen fast enough, not with a drunk holding a knife so close to her neck.

He went out the back door, pulled out his cell phone and keyed in 911. The bookmobile motor started, the doors closed and the vehicle moved slowly away from where Brian stood talking on the phone. They'd taken turns driving lately so she'd be able to make the routes during his occasional trips to California. Her cautious start and jerky movements now had to be a ruse to make the hijacker think she didn't know what she was doing. The vehicle moved forward at a crawl, slow enough for him to walk beside it while talking on the phone. He gave the 911 operator his location along with a quick summary of what was happening.

Suddenly, the mobile library shot forward with more speed before it stopped abruptly. Both doors flew open simultaneously. Brian jumped in the front door to find the hijacker on the floor. He grabbed her wrist and squeezed it until she released the weapon.

"Ouch," she said. "What are you doing? I told you I'm on a mission from God. You're hurting me. God, he's hurting me."

He smelled the alcohol and knew she was indeed under the control of spirits, just not the one she thought she was.

"It's good to talk to God, but as humans, we're fallible and we don't always understand what God is saying."

Karen stood next to him and for the first time since the woman boarded the bookmobile, had a big smile on her face.

After the police got there and took the woman into custody, Brian relaxed enough to tell Karen about his fear. "I don't want to hear any excuses, I'm hiring a security guard. I thought I was going to lose you."

"It's not necessary," she said. "I know who she is."

"You do? Who?"

She nodded toward the drunk in handcuffs being led away. "That's Cloris Parker."

CHAPTER FIFTEEN

Karen enjoyed the monthly bookmobile planning meetings with the director of library services. Brian considered all meetings a waste of time, and he reminded Karen of that today as they sat in Liz's office waiting for her to join them.

"You know," he said, "we could take care of all this business by e-mail."

"Probably," Karen said. "But then we wouldn't get a hug from Liz."

Brian snickered. "You're right about that."

Karen stifled a laugh.

"What?" Brian asked.

"I wonder if Liz is hugging everyone she sees now that she has a boyfriend."

"Oh, yeah. She hasn't changed a bit. The other day we were walking to the main library when some stranger stopped us and asked for directions to the courthouse. After telling him, Liz grabbed him and hugged him right there on the sidewalk. As soon as the man got out of her grip, he turned and ran."

Karen tried to hold back another chuckle when Liz walked in, her gray hair flew this way and that. As usual, her makeup was non-existent. Karen remembered how Virgil had been all spiffed up at the wedding reception and thought what an unusual couple they made.

"What's so funny?" Liz asked.

Karen and Brian stood and Karen grabbed Liz, initiating the hug before Liz for once.

"Nothing," Karen said. "We were just talking about what a great hugger you are."

Liz's eyes popped open, but she smiled and hugged Brian next.

Liz positioned three guest chairs in a circle. She sat in one and motioned for them to take the other two.

"How's Virgil?" Karen asked after they were seated.

Liz rewarded her with a wide smile. "Well, thank you for asking. He's just fine."

"Good," Karen said. "Tell him hello for us."

"I surely will." Liz's attitude turned more business-like. "I hear the bookmobile got hijacked yesterday."

"Yes," Brian said, "we did. But the hijacker didn't get far. Karen pretended she didn't know how to drive and the woman fell to the floor when Karen sped up a little then stomped on the brakes."

"Yes," Karen added. "And as soon as she fell, Brian jumped on board and grabbed her knife. He'd already called the cops, so it was over pretty quickly."

Liz stared at her for a few seconds as if waiting for Karen to say more. "You seem happy about something. What's going on?"

"It turns out the hijacker is the same woman who's suing me. I talked to Richard about it and he thinks this might be just what we need to get the lawsuit dropped."

"Well," Liz said, "let's hope it works. I know having that case hanging over your head must be hard for you."

"Thank you," Karen said.

"Now, let's get to work. Today's meeting is more important than usual," Liz said, looking at Karen and then Brian before continuing. "It's time to prepare the budget for the next fiscal year and I want to make sure we have a city-financed bookmobile in our request. You remember what happened last time, don't you?" She nodded to Brian.

"Yes," Brian said. "The council approved the idea of getting a bookmobile, but didn't budget for it."

Brian turned to Karen. "Liz set up a bookmobile fund to get donations. When she saw how much her new salary was, she started donating to the fund herself."

Karen frowned. "Aren't you providing the bookmobile service?"

"I am," Brian said. "I mean, we are. But Liz wants a city-owned bookmobile and she wants the city to recognize the importance of the service and pay for it. I promised Liz I'd do it for another year, and the year is ending soon."

"I see," Karen said.

"Yes," Liz said. "The city needs to pay for this, not you. The patrons love it. Ever since Brian brought the bookmobile back to Austin, we've had tons of requests from neighborhoods, rest homes, and businesses to be added to the route. We could use two bookmobiles if we had them, maybe three."

"Really?" Brian said. "I'm glad to hear that."

"Yes. So you can stay on as long as you like, even if we get our own."

"We hadn't talked about getting out of the bookmobile business any time soon," Karen said. "I enjoy it and I know Brian does, too."

"Good. I hope you like it enough to add a new stop."

"Sure," Brian said. He turned to Karen. "Right?"

"Yes," Karen said. "We have a free slot on Thursdays."

"Perfect," Liz said. "I've found a neighborhood of people living on government assistance. They're not close to any of our branch libraries and most of them don't have private transportation."

"Just give us an address and we'll start next week."

Liz handed Brian a piece of paper. "Here it is."

"How's the bookmobile fund doing?" Brian asked.

Liz smiled. "We have enough money in the bank to buy the vehicle. That's about a hundred and forty thousand dollars. I think the city would budget salaries for people to staff it, especially when they learn they don't have to pay for the bookmobile itself."

"What if the city decides to use the bookmobile fund for something else?" Brian asked.

"They can't. The donations are in a private account with my name on it. There's no taxpayer money involved. After I buy the vehicle, I'll give it to the city."

"Good idea," Brian said.

"Liz?"

All eyes turned toward the door where a tall muscular man in a black uniform stood.

Liz was on her feet faster than Karen imagined possible.

"Tom, come on in," Liz said as she walked to the door and grabbed him in a hug. "The chief of police is always welcome."

The chief came in and closed the door. "I hope I'm not interrupting anything. I need to talk to you alone, but I can come back after your meeting." He nodded toward Brian and Karen.

"No, it's okay. We had just finished. Right?" She looked at Brian before turning to Karen.

"Yes," Karen said.

"Tom, have you met Brian and Karen? These are the two people who stopped the bookmobile hijacking yesterday."

"I heard about that. Please accept my sincere appreciation. You two may have saved some lives by talking her out of driving the bookmobile and then quickly capturing her."

"Thank you," Karen said.

Brian nodded. They walked toward the door.

"You have my sincere thanks too," Liz said. "I'll send you a copy of the budget to review and get the newspaper to announce the new bookmobile stop and we'll put it on the library's Internet page." She hugged them both again before they left.

In the hall, Brian turned to Karen. "I could sure use some coffee."

"Me too."

"I'll load the bookmobile if you'll go across the street and get us some coffee to go."

"Agreed."

Karen went out the east door while Brian headed for the loading dock on the west side of the History Center.

***

Before their meeting with Liz, Brian had parked the bookmobile parallel to the library loading dock. A three-foot wide aluminum portable access ramp, similar to the ones that pull out of the tail of rental trucks, spanned the distance from the dock to the floor of the bookmobile at the vehicle's front door.

He placed the box of books he and Karen had selected for today's run on the checkout table and pulled the first book out to be shelved. He smiled when he saw one of the older Bonnie Hearn Hill books staring back at him. Just as he slid it into the shelf with the other thrillers, he heard what sounded like someone knocking outside the bookmobile. He glanced out, but saw no one. He took another book to shelve when he heard the sound again, louder this time and sounding as if it came from the top of the vehicle. He crossed the ramp to the loading dock and looked up. Liz's boyfriend, Virgil Golden, peeked over the top just above where Brian stood on the ramp.

"Virgil? What are you doing up there? We're getting ready to leave."

Virgil shook his head.

"Is that a handkerchief in your mouth?"

Virgil nodded and mumbled something that didn't make sense.

Brian found a chair on the dock. He put it in the middle of the ramp close to the bookmobile entrance. He climbed up to where he could reach Virgil and pulled the handkerchief out of Virgil's mouth. "What's going on?" Brian said, looking around the area cautiously. He climbed off the chair and stood on the aluminum ramp. "I'll hold the chair for you to climb down to."

"Can't," said Virgil.

"Can't what?"

"Can't get down."

"Sure you can. Just turn around and come feet first. Grab that edge rail on the top of the bookmobile and let yourself down onto the chair."

"Can't. My hands are tied behind my back, you idiot. Don't you think I would've pulled that thing out of my mouth if I could have? Besides, I don't have any clothes on."

"What?"

"I'm naked. NAKED! Are you deaf or something?"

"Where are your clothes?"

Virgil nodded toward the library. "Ask him."

Brian turned around to see Tex sitting in his wheelchair, with his six-gallon hat perched at an angle, watching and grinning. He must have rolled out while Brian talked to Virgil.

Tex held out his palms and shrugged.

"He's in a wheelchair," Brian said. "He couldn't have taken your clothes."

"Not him. Those ex-con friends of his. Jimbo and that other guy. They took my clothes, tied me up and put me up here. He told them to do it."

Tex shrugged again, but this time his accompanying smile turned the response from "Who me?" to a "Maybe," making Brian wonder what was going on.

From what Brian knew, Tex worshipped Liz. So why would he hurt her boyfriend? Brian shook his head and climbed back up on the chair. "Okay, turn around to where I can reach the rope. Once I untie you, I want you to get down."

"You can untie me, but I'm not coming down without my clothes on. Otherwise, I'll get into trouble with the law."

"Seems to me you're already in trouble." Brian untied him, trying his best not to touch the lily white skin of the man's backside.

"Tex, where are his clothes?" Brian asked as he climbed down off the chair.

Tex shrugged again.

Tex's response irritated Brian. He wanted to get Virgil down and dressed before Karen showed up.

"Well, do you have anything in lost and found he can cover up with?"

Tex chuckled. "Maybe a hat or a coat. Not many people go off and forget their pants in the library."

"We need to get him down," Brian said. "Karen will be back in a minute and I don't want her to see him. If fact, no one should have to see what I saw while untying him."

"A homeless man poked around here a while back," Tex said. "He was tickled to death when he found a nice set of clothes on the loading dock. He put them on and thanked me.

"You knew that was my clothes he took."

"Me?" Tex said.

"So what you're saying is Virgil's clothes are gone," Brian said.

"Yep," Tex said. "But the gentleman who took them was kind enough to leave his old clothes."

Brian scanned the area. "Where? I don't see any clothes."

"They stunk so bad I asked him to put them in the dumpster." Tex pointed to where the trash bin stood open in the corner of the parking lot.

"You just happened to watch all this?" Brian said.

"Well, I thought someone might need to know."

"But you didn't try to stop it?"

Tex tapped the wheelchair handles with both hands. "How could I stop anything from happening while sitting in this thing?"

"I know you're involved," Brian said. "You can deny it all you want, but clearly you're behind what happened here. Why? I thought you liked Liz. Why would you want to hurt her?"

"I love Liz," Tex said. "That's why someone would do this. To protect her."

Virgil groaned. "Oh, please."

Brian ignored Virgil. "Has Virgil hurt her?"

"Not yet," Tex said. "But it was just a matter of time."

"How do you know?" Brian asked.

"That's bull," Virgil said. "I'd never hurt her."

"He'd break her heart for sure," Tex said. "He's a con man. He goes about the country looking for places where he can volunteer and not have to have a background check. As soon as he gets on the boss's good side he steals everything he can put his hands on. He's wanted in several states. Someone needed to stop him before he hurt Liz."

"And how do you know this?" Brian asked.

"I'll tell you later," Tex said.

"Does Liz know about him?" Brian nodded toward Virgil.

Tex checked his watch. "Probably. We talked to the police and the chief, who is a personal friend of Liz's, was supposed to meet with her this morning and tell her all about Virgil."

Virgil groaned. "Get me down now, quick. I don't want to talk to no police. I'm naked here, you know."

"Hold your horses," Brian said. "I saw the police chief with Liz just before I came down here. What do you think? Should we get this creep some clothes or leave him there in case Liz wants to say good bye."

"Get me down!" Virgil said. "Please." It was almost a scream.

"As much as I'm enjoying this," Tex said, "I don't think Virgil should be here when Liz gets out of her meeting with the chief. For her sake."

"I agree," said Brian. "You say there are some clothes in the trash bin?"

"Yes. Take the broom with you to dip them out so you won't have to climb in or touch any of those rags. The clothes I saw tossed away were as worn out as they were soiled."

Brian took the broom he used to sweep out the bookmobile and walked to the dumpster. He leaned into the rubble and saw a pile of what could be clothes. Using the handle end of the broom, he snagged a grimy-looking shirt and pair of holey pants. The smell of body odor mixed with urine reached his nose. Swinging the handle like a baseball bat, he propelled the clothes up to Virgil.

Virgil dressed quickly and climbed down to the chair. From there, he jumped off the ramp and ran toward Shoal Creek without saying a word or looking back. He was out of sight in a matter of seconds.

"Now," Brian said. "You were going to tell me how you learned Virgil is a con man."

Tex took off his cowboy hat and pushed his hair back with one hand. "You know that situation you asked us to look into?"

Brian nodded. "I asked you to find out who was stalking Karen and me."

"That's what I'm talking about. We were investigating the Cloris woman when Virgil showed up."

"What? Virgil and Cloris are connected? How?

Tex put his hat on. "We've got photos of them together. In one of them, they're kissing. That's how they're connected. Right at the lips."

"Liz is going to be mad. I think she actually liked him. She usually can read people better than that. He must be a real con man to fool her."

"I know," Tex said. "I thought the same thing. After we saw him with Cloris, we did a background check and found he has taken advantage of women before, especially those in nonprofit organizations."

"At least you found out before he hurt her."

"It's going to hurt, but at least he didn't steal anything that we know of. I don't guess he's the one who stalked you in Germany and Bruges," Tex asked.

"No. The guy we saw was much younger. Besides, we would have recognized Virgil. He came to the wedding with Liz."

Tex straightened his hat. "I thought so. Be careful, though. I find it strange that someone connected to Karen's lawsuit gets this close to Liz. That's not coincidental, you know."

Brian wondered how Tex had gotten a naked Virgil on top of the bookmobile. "No, it's not. Good job, by the way. I don't want to know how you did it, but if he was planning to hurt Liz, he deserved what he got. Getting him into those dirty clothes was a nice touch, especially since he's always dressed so nicely. I just wish I knew more about his connection with Cloris."

"What about Cloris?" Karen asked as she walked up carrying a cardboard tray with two cups of steaming coffee.

CHAPTER SIXTEEN

After dinner the following Monday, Karen decided it was time to find the shoebox. Brian had helped in the kitchen and now sat in front of his computer talking to one of his managers in the California company. Karen got his attention and he put the call on hold.

"I'm going to run over to the Sunset Valley house and look for the shoebox," she said.

"Shoebox?"

"I told you about that. Remember? The box full of trinkets and stuff Ernest left that might be important to the lawsuit."

"Oh, yeah. Do you want me to go with you?"

"No. You're busy. I won't be long."

When she arrived at her house, out of habit, she drove her car into the garage and shut the door before going into the house. The place looked about the same as when she moved to Brian's house. All her furniture was there and the kitchen was fully supplied. She'd moved clothing and necessities to her new home, but compared to what was left, it was hardly noticeable. She planned to sell the house eventually, but she wasn't in a hurry. She and Julie needed to go through everything and decide what to keep and what to move.

Tonight, Karen's goal was to find the shoebox. First, she walked through the house, a room at a time, trying to trigger her memory of where it could be. Not getting vibes, she started with the hall closet and searched it thoroughly. That was the place they stored things that weren't used often. It included some items that should be thrown out, but were saved just in case. Rolls of Christmas wrapping paper, broken umbrellas, and long unused suitcases caught her eye when she opened the door. She pulled out the suitcases and examined each one carefully. Nothing. She probably should throw out unneeded items as she identified them, but if she did she'd be there all night. She'd save that job for another time. Maybe when Julie was here to help, or at least tell her what she wanted to keep. She went to the guest bedroom closet next.

Digging around in twenty something years of possessions no longer needed wasn't fun. Each closet in the house contained memories. Just not the ones she was looking for. Some were good, but many weren't. There were bits and pieces of Steve in the house even though they'd divorced more than three years ago. After plowing through the last closet, she vowed to come back on a Saturday and clean house, with or without Julie.

It was past ten by the time she remembered to look at her watch. She decided she'd better call Brian. Ever since Cloris tried to hijack the bookmobile, he'd been on edge. Before she had a chance to pull out her cell phone, it rang. She smiled, thinking Brian had read her mind and was calling to check on her. But it wasn't Brian. The call was from a number she didn't recognize and instead of the caller's name, the word "unknown" was shown. She didn't usually answer calls like that but she thought it might be Julie calling on a friend's phone.

"Hello," she said, cautiously.

"Listen carefully." It sounded like the man who called when Harriet had the phone. The one with the slight English accent.

Her heart pounded so hard she feared she wouldn't be able to hear what he said next. She took a deep breath and waited.

"If you care about your daughter's safety, you will find a reason to stay out of court. Do you understand?"

Julie. Safety. Court. She took another breath to calm her nervousness. "Who is this?" she asked.

"This is the person warning you to butt out." He spat out the last two words.

She felt like he was in the room with her, but that wasn't possible. She couldn't help turning around just in case. "I don't know what you're talking about," Karen said. "Are you sure you have the right phone number?"

There was a brief silence. "Is this Karen Williams Donelson?"

"Yes."

"Then I have the right number."

She rubbed the back of her neck. Was something crawling on her? "Okay. But I don't understand what you want me to do."

"If you're trying to play dumb while you trace this call, don't bother. This phone is untraceable."

"I'm hanging up and calling the police. We'll see if they can trace the call or not."

"You think you're so smart, don't you. Well, it won't work. Listen up. I'm only going to say this once. Drop the complaint against the woman you claim hijacked the bookmobile and settle with the woman who sued you."

She wanted to run. She turned slowly making a complete turn while she scanned the room again. She was alone, but she felt evil around her, close by.

"Aren't they the same person?" Karen asked.

There was another silence on the line. "Just do it."

"And if I don't?"

"Then Julie may disappear."

Karen's heartbeat was audible and the fear she felt was stronger than any she'd ever felt. The fear turned to anger in an instant. "Listen here, you touch my daughter and you'll answer to me." She wanted to say something more, something stronger, but the dial tone stopped her.

Her first thought was to call the police. But she could do that from home. She didn't want to hang around here waiting for the police to show up. She had to call Julie right away. She could be in danger. Her daughter didn't answer until the fifth ring.

"Where are you?" Karen asked.

"I'm here. Amy's. Why?"

"When you didn't answer, I got worried."

"Mom, I had to go find my phone. If it had been too long it would have gone to voicemail. What's wrong?"

"Nothing. Just wanted to talk. Is Amy home?"

"No. She's in California."

"So you're there alone?" An idea to get Julie into a more protective environment came to Karen as she talked.

"Yes."

"I'd like for you to go stay at your dad's for a while."

"What? Why?"

"He needs babysitting help. You can study when the kids are asleep."

"He didn't say anything to me about it when I talked to him the other day."

That was because Karen hadn't told him yet. "Something just came up. He was going to call you tomorrow."

"Well, okay. I like spending time with the kids. Plus, I won't have to cook."

"You'll do it then?"

"Yes."

"Good. I'll tell him. Goodnight, sweetie. Love you."

Karen called Steve next.

"Hello," he said. "Do you know what time it is?"

"Sorry if I woke you. This is important. I need a favor without having to answer too many questions."

"Okay. What?"

"I want you to call Julie first thing tomorrow and ask her to stay at your place a week or so to help with the kids."

"Well, that's easy. Consider it done."

"I also need to tell you to watch her closely. You know about this lawsuit I'm involved in, right?"

"A little. I was surprised to learn you'd been married before."

"Yeah, sorry about that. Anyway, this thing is getting messy and I want to make sure Julie doesn't get hurt because of it."

"Are you saying you've received threats?"

She had to tell him for Julie's sake. "Yes. I'm not sure if they would hurt Julie to get to me, but I don't want to take a chance on it."

"Well, don't worry. They'll have to get past me first."

'Thanks. Don't alarm her, though. I haven't said anything to her about it, only that you need some help watching the kids."

"No sweat. Actually, we're off work next week and were planning a car trip to the gulf coast. Julie could probably skip a week of classes and go with us."

Since their breakup Steve had grown into a decent father. Too bad it took a divorce and new family to get him there.

The threatening phone call scared her more than she let on to the creep on the other end of the line. Even though he'd hung up on her, she still felt he was nearby. Then, she knew he was. As soon as she drove away from her house someone in a black pickup truck pulled out and followed her. She watched the truck in her rearview mirror as it matched her turn for turn from Sunset Valley to Ben White Boulevard. When she'd acted so strong talking to him she had no idea he was that nearby. If, of course, it was the caller behind her in the pickup and if the vehicle was in deed following. Paranoia had been known to distort facts.

The route from her Sunset Valley house to Brian's house took her onto the MoPac freeway for a few miles before turning off on 35th Street. The black pickup stayed with her turn for turn.

When the truck took the turn to the west on 35th Street, it was time to formulate a plan about what to do. She could call the police, but what would she tell them? Could she out run him? She knew the roads around Mount Bonnell. He might not. Still, it would be dangerous zooming around in the hills. If she could get home, inside the gates, she'd be safe. All she had to do was call Brian so he could help her get through the gates in a hurry. She grabbed her phone and called him.

"Hi. Are you almost home?" he asked.

"Listen. I'll explain later. I'm being followed by a black pickup. I want you to open the gate for me and then shut it as soon as I drive through. Understand?" Her heartbeat increased as she held the phone in one hand and the steering wheel in the other. Don't let him ask questions. Not now.

"Got it. Where are you now?" His voice was strong and reassuring. She relaxed knowing he'd be there to help.

"I'm just starting down the hill from Mount Bonnell."

"The gate will be open and I'll close it after you. Be safe."

At least he didn't ask why she was being followed. She clicked off and grabbed the steering wheel with both hands. She glanced out her left window and saw the pickup beside her. What was he doing now? He could block her from turning left into the driveway. The window was so heavily tinted she couldn't see the driver. The truck continued on around until it was in front of her. Could it be he wasn't following her after all? Perhaps he would pass her and go on his way.

The feeling of relief didn't last long. As soon as the truck was in front of her, it started slowing. The pickup's brake lights glowed brightly, spasmodically, as the truck got closer to her front bumper. She hit her brakes to put more distance between them. Doing so allowed the pickup to slow more. She tried to pass but the truck swerved with her to block her from going around.

There was a deep gully on the right and drop off on the left. Stopping would be the last resort. She had to find a way to go around the truck or keep moving forward until she got to her driveway. Did the driver of the pickup know where she was going? It wasn't far now, but she was being forced to slow so much, she was afraid she'd never make it home. Suddenly, a car came toward them forcing the truck to move to the right. When it did, Karen gunned it and went around the pickup knowing there would be little room for the maneuver. But she had no choice. Her turnoff was coming up quickly. The oncoming car jerked to its right with its horn blaring and gravel from the road's shoulder flying, but Karen passed the pickup and turned into her driveway before the truck could catch up to her.

The driver of the pickup recovered quickly and was on her tail sooner than she thought possible. She wanted to call Brian and warn him. He could be hurt if the pickup was so close behind her. She felt around on the car seat where her phone should be, but found nothing. It must have fallen off the seat during the stops and turns. The driveway to the house was about five hundred feet long with a curve two-thirds the way in and a gate near the cabin. When she got past the curve she didn't need to call him. Brian stood with the gate open for her with a shotgun cradled over one arm. She prayed no one would get hurt. She zipped through the gate just far enough for Brian to shut it and stopped. Through her back window she could see Brian standing in the middle of the driveway with the gate closed and the shotgun pointed at the pickup.

"Don't shoot," she said, too softly for him to hear.

She listened for the blast but she heard burning rubber instead. She watched the pickup back up at full speed and turn into some trees near the curve in the driveway and hightail it off the Donelson property.

She got out of the car and ran to Brian, wanting his arms around her to protect her and his strength to calm her. He glanced back up the driveway one more time before he opened the shotgun and removed shells from both barrels. Leaving the barrels open, he held her in one arm, and the gun in the other. She nestled there until her heart beat returned to normal. Only then did she let go of him. He put the gun in the backseat of the car and drove her the rest of the way to the house.

"We need to call the police," he said as soon as they were on the way. "Did you happen to get a license number?"

"No. I was too busy trying to stay on the road. I think he wanted to kill me." She sounded frantic, but she didn't care. The ordeal was scary.

He had both hands on the steering wheel looking straight ahead. "It was black, right?"

Brian parked the car and recovered the shotgun. They walked to the house hand in hand. She felt better with each step, but she'd never forget what could have happened.

"Yes," she said. "Definitely black. He followed me all the way from Sunset Valley."

"What? Why didn't you call sooner? I could've gotten the police to help. They could have been here waiting for him."

His question made her uncomfortable. "I didn't know he was following me for sure until I turned onto 35th Street, and even then it could have been coincidental. My plan was to get home and have you meet me at the gate. I accomplished that. Don't ask me why I didn't do something else. I made it home."

Anger crept into her body and she didn't know why. She had no reason to be mad at Brian.

"I'm sorry," he said. "I'm just trying to find out what happened."

Brian put the gun away and made a phone call.

"Tex, this is Brian. Karen was followed home tonight and the driver of a black pickup tried to run her off the road."

Brian paused.

"She didn't get a license number. I pointed a shotgun at the truck when it got here and it left in a hurry."

Another pause.

"Okay. Thanks." Brian put his phone away.

"Tex said he'd get someone to look around, but he said the truck probably wouldn't hang around long after seeing I was armed."

Suddenly overcome with exhaustion, Karen flopped onto the sofa in the family room.

Brian sat next to her. "Can you tell me anything else about the driver. Did you see his face? Was he young, old, anything unusual about him?"

"The truck's windows were so tinted I couldn't see anyone."

"Figures."

"Oh, I think he was the same person who called me."

"What? He phoned you?"

"I'm not sure," she said. "I got a call earlier tonight from a man who didn't give his name. He told me to drop the criminal case and settle the civil case."

"Or what?"

"Or Julie would disappear."

"He said that?" Brian stood, getting his phone out again. "Did you call the police?"

"Now, just wait," she said. "I took care of it. I talked to Julie and she's going on a trip with her dad and his family. She'll be safe."

"Are you sure? What about Amy? What if they go looking for Julie at Amy's and take her instead?"

"Amy's in California. She didn't tell you?"

"No. Yes, I think she did and I forgot when she was going."

"She'll be safe there."

"Did you tell Julie why you wanted her to hide out?"

"No, but I told Steve and asked him to tell her if he thinks it's necessary."

"Okay," Brian said, pacing. "That's good. We can hire security guards to watch you and her around the clock. I'll call Amy to see when she plans to be back in Austin and warn her about what's going on." He took his phone out again. "Maybe Tex can track down who called your cell phone."

"Can that be done?"

"I don't know, but we need to try."

"You can call Amy and ask her whether she'd feel safer with guards, but I don't want anyone else following me. These are just scare tactics. I don't think they would actually carry out the threat."

"You didn't think that a few minutes ago. You said you thought he was trying to kill you. And you're right. That pickup could have run you off the side of the road and, if it had, you could have rolled all the way down to the lake. And there's no telling what would have happened if I hadn't aimed my shotgun at his windshield."

"The maneuvers on the road scared me. But now that I've had time to think about it and the phone call, I believe he was just trying to scare me, that's all."

"Well he sure scared me," Brian said. "Besides, it doesn't matter how serious the threat was. We need to report it. Since the caller mentioned the court case, maybe Richard can use another legal action against them to get them to drop the lawsuit." Brian looked at his watch. "Let's call Richard and tell him all about what happened and let him take it from there. I'll call Ron in the morning and get a security team to watch you."

"No."

Brian stopped in mid-step. "No?"

"No. If I live my life with guards watching over me around the clock then Cloris has already won. I don't need help with this. I handled the situation tonight. I'm glad you were here to open the gate and stop the pickup, but if you hadn't been here, I would have done something else. I'm not helpless."

Brian had his mouth open, ready to respond, when his phone rang. He pulled it out of his pants pocket and answered it.

"Hi, Dad," Brian said. "No, I'm awake. Is everything okay? What? I can't hear you. Hold on a minute."

He pulled the phone away from his ear and turned to Karen. "Reception's bad here, I'm going upstairs and see if I can get a better connection. I'll be right back."

He put the instrument back to his ear. "Are you there? Just a minute. I'm walking to a spot where I can hear you better."

Karen turned on the teapot and got out cups for both of them. When Brian's father called it was usually bad news about his mother. Mrs. Donelson had Alzheimer's and was getting worse. Mr. Donelson nearly wore himself out caring for her until Brian stepped in and got around-the-clock care for her. She hoped his mother was okay, but...was it right to wish comfort for someone in her condition? And by comfort she meant God's comfort.

She carried the cups to the patio and paused on the dock, taking in the beauty of the moonlight rippling on the water. She glanced up to the second floor to see if Brian was there. He wasn't. She turned back to see him walking toward her. Something was wrong.

"We have a great view here," he said, looking beyond her to the creek with the moonlight reflecting on it.

"So? Your mother?" she asked.

"Yes."

"Did she...?"

"No, no." He shook his head and took Karen in his arms and held her close.

She felt his heartbeat.

"She's worse. The home nurse care team recommended she be admitted to a special facility for advanced Alzheimer's patients. They wouldn't do that unless it was needed."

"How's your dad taking it?"

"Not good. Oh, he accepts the fact Mom needs to be moved to a place where she can get special care. But he's so drained, mentally and physically, I don't think he can manage it alone."

"You need to be there," Karen said.

"I can't leave you here. Not now."

Karen hugged him. "Do you want me to come, too?"

"Yes. I'd love that."

"Okay. I have to be in court. Why don't you take the early flight tomorrow and I'll join you the next day."

"Can't Richard change the court date?"

"Maybe, but we've been waiting a month for it. Tell Liz I'll drive the bookmobile to the library early Wednesday morning so they can use it while we're gone."

"I'm sure they could send someone to pick it up," Brian said.

"It's no problem."

CHAPTER SEVENTEEN

Brian parked the rental car at the curb in front of his parent's Redondo Beach home. The drive from the LA airport had left him exhausted. He thought Austin drivers were difficult, but only because he'd forgotten how crowded the roads were in the Los Angeles area. Not that Californians were bad drivers. They were just always in such a hurry.

He turned off the engine and sat with his forehead on the steering wheel to unwind. He thought about his mother, trying to remember the last time they'd talked. The last time she knew who he was. That was the hardest part. Knowing she no longer recognized him. Alzheimer's gradually took the patient's life, but it changed the patient's family in ways Brian found difficult to comprehend.

It was time to take her to a place where she would get around-the-clock care and where she might be happy. Maybe then his dad would be able to sleep all night again. Even with around the clock help at home, his dad jumped out of bed every time his mother was upset or needed something.

It was time to go in. Brian reached for his cell phone to turn off the ringer. He noticed he had a new e-mail from Liz. He opened it and read the brief message. "Is this the guy?" Three photos were attached, all of a young-looking man walking across a street. In the first, he stood between two parked cars at the edge of the street with his head turned slightly to his right. The second image showed him in full stride, halfway across the street, looking left. The third picture was a full portrait of the man as he stepped up on the curb on the other side of the street.

Brian enlarged the image around the man's face on each of the three pictures. There was no question about it. These were photos of their stalker. He wouldn't easily forget the man he'd seen in Bruges and again in the bookmobile. He scrolled down to the end of the message, but found no mention of who the man was. He tapped in a quick response. "Yes. Who?"

He was going to sit in the car and wait for Liz to respond until he realized how silly that was. He switched over to the phone app and called her.

She picked up on the first ring. "I thought you might call. The man in the photos is Heath Brower. Karen's stepson."

"Are you sure?"

"Yes. Of course. Chris and Tex took the pictures."

"Did you tell Karen?" He wanted to be the one to tell her and he wasn't sure if he'd made that clear to Liz and the guys when they met.

"No. I'll leave that to you."

"Thanks. And thank the guys for me."

"Sure. They were glad to have a way to repay you for all you've done for them."

"All I did was throw money at problems." He grimaced. Karen told him he was good at that.

"I know, but that was what was needed. Chris probably wouldn't have been able to recover from his fiancée's death without your help. Tex wouldn't be at the University of Texas without the scholarships you provided. And don't forget how loaning them your bookmobile when you did saved the life of the President of the United States."

"I haven't forgotten, but it was because of you and the guys, not me or the bookmobile. By the way, how are you doing?"

"I'm fine."

"I'm talking about Virgil."

"I know you are and I'm still fine. Good riddance."

Brian could tell by the way her voice cracked she wasn't over it. Maybe he could ask Karen to talk to her, or listen to her the way she did with Harriet in Bruges. Listening was Karen's special gift.

They said good bye, but Brian didn't get out of the car. Even though his dad was expecting him, Brian needed time to consider what Liz had told him. In a way he was glad the stalker hadn't turned out to be someone connected to his ex-wife. He hadn't wanted to talk to her ever again, not since Amy told him the trick Judy had played to get him to marry her. He knew he was supposed to forgive Judy, but he wasn't ready to go that far.

He'd thought for sure the former owners of his company were the ones responsible for the stalker instead of Karen's stepson. Stepson was a word that tasted sour in his mouth. It didn't make sense for Heath to follow them to Germany and Belgium, and even less sense for him to walk into the bookmobile and pretend to be there to check out books. What was he planning to do with photographs of them? Or was that his ruse as a tourist? Of course it didn't make sense for Cloris to try to hijack the bookmobile or to sue Karen for that matter.

Brian stared at the photos, wondering if the kid was stupid or cunning. Was he the one who'd threatened her? Was he the driver of the black pickup?

Brian bowed his head and asked for help. "God, I love Karen dearly and would gladly take the pain to keep her from experiencing it. Watch over her now and throughout the trial she's facing."

The prayer gave him comfort, but he knew he had to call her. With his record of withholding information from her in the past and all the problems it caused, he had to tell her right away what he'd learned from Liz.

"Hi, honey," she said when she answered. "How's your dad?"

"I don't know. I haven't seen him yet."

"What? I thought you'd be there by now. Is everything okay?"

"Yes. I'm parked in front of the house. I checked my e-mail before going in and learned something I need to tell you."

"Oh? What?"

Brian wished he'd told her about meeting with Liz and her friends. He'd rationalized not saying anything to Karen by telling himself he didn't want to hurt her. But she preferred to know what was going on no matter what. Now he had to apologize once more for not sharing with her right away. "Honey, I'm sorry I didn't tell you before, but I asked Liz to use her contacts to help identify the young man who followed us."

"It was Heath," Karen said.

"Yes, I know you've believed that from the beginning. You'll be happy to know you were right. Now we know for sure it was Heath Brower who followed us. There were three photos attached to the email I got from Liz and I could see it was him."

"I know. I have a confession for you, too. I asked Richard and Cathy to help find out for sure and both of them came up with photos of Heath, too. With what they sent me and what Liz sent you we can start a family photo album, and we have yet to meet him. Officially, anyway." She laughed, but it wasn't her best laugh.

"And you're okay with this?"

She paused just long enough for Brian to be concerned.

"To be honest," she said, "I'm relieved. I thought it was him, but knowing takes away the doubts. What I'm curious about now is why. Also, I wonder if he followed us at other times and we didn't see him. Is he crazy? Is he dangerous? Did he call and threaten me? Was he driving the black pickup?"

"I know. I wondered about all that also. He could be dangerous. Still, I don't think he'd do anything to jeopardize the case against you. In fact, what we know about him could probably be used against him. Did you ask Richard about it?"

"I did. Richard said we can use Cloris's bookmobile hijacking against her, but he doesn't think we can pin anything on Heath. Not yet, anyway. Calling him a stalker doesn't make him one. All he's done is turn up in some unusual places at the same time we were there, but he hasn't threatened us. In fact, he could report you for chasing him off the bookmobile."

"He's a stalker. Did you tell Richard about the phone threat and the truck chasing you?"

"Yes. He's reporting both to the police and he contacted Cloris's lawyer about it."

"Good," Brian said. "Did you make your flight arrangements yet?"

"Yes. I'm all set. I have an early flight tomorrow. I'll e-mail you my arrival info."

"Good. I'll pick you up at the airport and we'll make this a mini-vacation. It'll let you forget about Heath and black pickups for a while."

"Sounds good. Don't forget I have to be in court today."

"I know. I'll talk to you tonight about it."

"I talked to Liz and told her I'd leave the bookmobile at the library if she'd give me a ride from there to the airport. She agreed and was happy about it."

"She should be. I still think you should have asked her to send someone out to get the bookmobile."

"I don't mind doing it this way. Otherwise, we'd have two cars at the airport. Hey. Did I tell you I miss you?"

"And I miss you, too," he said. "Be careful with the bookmobile. I parked it fairly close to the gulley."

"I will. Quit worrying so much."

"Guess I better say good bye and get in the house before Dad sends the sheriff out to find me. Love you."

"Love you, too."

***

The next morning Karen had her morning tea on the dock before the heat of the October day arrived. A slight breeze came in off the water, making it cooler than usual for seven o'clock in the morning. She had her prayer list with her, but, as often was the case, she didn't look at it. She knew the names by heart. Holding the crinkled paper was more of a ritual than a necessity. Even after making changes to the list from time to time she quickly memorized the new names.

Brian was number one on the list and she requested additional care for him today since he was away and because what he had to do was difficult for him. After going down the list of names, she finished her tea and took her cup to the kitchen. Realizing her prayers weren't over, she bowed at the kitchen sink and added a special prayer for herself.

"Dear God, help me do your will. This lawsuit is gnawing at me more and more each day. Now that I know Heath is the one who followed us, I don't know what to do. I'm innocent and I want to fight the case. But how can I be sure that's the right thing to do? It would be simpler if I accepted their offer to settle. Help me, Lord."

Karen stayed in her prayerful position for another minute, listening, as she always did. When she was open to a response from God, she was often rewarded with a special insight or a pearl of wisdom that might be a reply. But not today.

Karen dressed for her trip to California and packed her carryon. She remembered her promise to drive the bookmobile to the library, and began to go through a mental checklist. The vehicle was big and bulky and needed extra power at times. She remembered the steep incline of Mount Bonnell Road and how she'd have to negotiate it immediately after coming out of the driveway. After checking for traffic from the left she'd have to stomp on the accelerator to get enough speed to climb the hill. This would be her first time to drive alone, but she'd watched Brian do it many times, often describing to her what he was doing. He was a patient teacher. During her test drives, Brian had told her to always gun it at the base of every hill because the vehicle was so heavy and slow to build up speed.

She locked the house, opened the gate and rolled her carryon to the mobile library. Brian had left it facing out of the driveway, but had moved it far to the right to give room for their cars to get past. To the right of the bookmobile was a sudden drop off that led down to the water. It was covered with weeds and a few small mesquite trees. Karen placed her suitcase behind the driver's seat and climbed into the bookmobile. She glanced out the window on her right. All she could see was thick brush between her and the creek. She sat in the driver's seat, adjusted it, fastened her seat belt and, with the parking brake on and the gears in neutral, turned on the engine. She rotated the steering wheel to the left to make sure she'd pull away from the chasm. She stepped on the brake, pushed the clutch to the floorboard, and put it in first gear. She let out the clutch slowly while stepping on the accelerator. The bookmobile jerked slightly but the engine died before the vehicle moved forward.

She checked and found she'd forgotten to release the parking brake. She stepped on the brake pedal and turned the parking brake handle to disengage it. With the clutch in and her foot firmly on the brake pedal, she started the engine again. She made sure the vehicle was in first gear before she moved her right foot quickly from the brake pedal to the accelerator as she slowly let up on the clutch. The bookmobile moved forward slightly just before it fell sharply to the right. She jerked the steering wheel to the left while pressing harder on the accelerator thinking the steering wheel would turn easier while the vehicle was moving.

Instead, the bookmobile continued to fall to the right. She hit the brakes, but nothing changed. Her heart raced as she tightened her grip on the steering wheel. The vehicle rolled over on its right side, into the scrub trees. The seatbelt kept her from falling out of her seat.

"Oh, piffle," Karen said as the strap of the belt pulled against her shoulders, then her waist, then her shoulders again. In a matter of seconds she was upside down, tied to the vehicle by the seatbelt and her grip on the steering wheel. Her arm muscles were strained to their limits as she held tight, not trusting the seat belts. She screamed. The pull on her body changed again and her body settled back into the seat. Books fell with her. Her suitcase flopped from side to side. Another turn, another jerk, another scream. With each rotation the bookmobile picked up speed. She wondered if the bookmobile would float.

***

Brian had selected the Twilight Meadows Care Facility in Redondo Beach, California, for his mother because it offered the best care for Alzheimer's patient's money could buy.

The move would be better for his mother and his father, he told himself as he pushed her wheelchair toward the ramp leading to the front door of the home where she would most likely spend the rest of her life. Tears came to his eyes as he acknowledged her pending death.

He remembered the last time he'd talked to her before she climbed into that unknown world of hers and shut the door permanently, back when she knew who he was. She'd not acted sad. Her concern was for her family. She'd told them what was happening, but neither he nor his dad had wanted to accept it. Thinking about that conversation now, he knew they were doing what she would want.

"Where's Amy?" his dad asked. "She's in town, isn't she?"

"She is. She has a board meeting to go to. She'll be here later today to visit with Mom."

His dad grabbed Brian's arm and stopped him. "Are we doing the right thing?"

Brian brushed at his eyes with his sleeve, strangely aware they were talking in front of his mother. "Dad, we've been through this before. I still think this is best for Mom. I realize how hard it is for you. It's not easy for me either. You still okay with it?"

"I guess. I don't know what else to do. I can't care for her at home any longer, even with the help." He looked at his wife sitting quietly holding a blanket on her lap. "I just wish she could tell us for sure this is what she wants."

"I know. Me too. We'll probably never know. We have to do what we think is best for her. She needs more care now. She's having problems eating and drinking. This place knows how to deal with all the special difficulties patients have. We don't."

"You're right. Still, like you said, it's hard." His dad looked worn out.

Brian started pushing her again, moving slowly toward the door that would take his mother into a new world and away from her home with his father, the home where Brian grew up.

Brian learned from the administrator that some patients lived for years in Twilight Meadows Care Facility while others were only there for a month or so. Some patients improved at first because of the change of diet. Others are stimulated by activities and their lives take on new meaning and they're happier than before. But none are cured. All eventually get worse. They couldn't promise Martha would be happier, but they did promise to take good care of her.

A young man in a light blue nurse's uniform came out to meet them. "Here, let me help," he said, taking the wheelchair from Brian.

Brian didn't resist and moved around to where he could see his mother's face. She stared straight ahead, apparently without noticing him or her surroundings. No reaction to what was going on. *Did she know she was moving? Was she afraid? What was she thinking?* Her face offered no clues.

Brian's phone rang and he wished he'd turned it off. He checked the screen and saw it was Liz. Since they weren't inside the care facility yet, he took the call. "Hello, Liz. What's up?"

"Karen's not with you is she?" Liz asked.

"Uh...no. Not yet. I don't expect her until late this afternoon."

"She told me she was driving the bookmobile in to the library and would need a ride to the airport."

"Yeah, that's what she told me, too." Brian didn't like the way the conversation was going. He felt his heartbeat rise. Something was wrong. "She's not there yet?" He checked the time.

"No. I've called her cell several times, but she doesn't answer.

"That's weird. Let me try to call her and I'll get back to you."

"Brian, wait. There's more. I knew you were out of town so I sent someone out to the house to see if she was there."

Brian's mind raced as he considered possibilities for what could have happened to her. "That's good. I'll try to call, but let me know when you hear something."

"I will. It's probably nothing, but with all this stuff about Heath and the lawsuit, I felt we should look into it."

"Thanks, Liz. Call me."

Heath wouldn't dare do anything to hurt her. Stalking her and letting the air out of her tires were bad enough, but would he actually hurt her? Yes–if he'd been the one who tried to run her off the road. Was he unbalanced like his mother? He'd have to be to do what he'd done.

Brian pressed Karen's name from his favorite's list on his phone and let it ring until it went to voicemail. He left a short message, hung up and called again. Still no answer. He called the house phone, too, leaving a message there as well. All he could do now was wait until Karen or Liz called back.

They checked his mother into the facility and followed her to her room. She got out of the wheelchair and walked across the room to her sofa, the one they'd had delivered from home. It was where she sat most often and she seemed to recognize it right away. She looked sad and less alert than usual. Her gray hair was flat, almost pasted to her scalp. Before her illness, she had always fluffed her hair up high on her head. Always the example of perfect posture, now she sat slump-shouldered. At least she didn't seem frightened the way she did from time to time since the illness started. That was something to be thankful for. Perhaps she will be happier here.

Brian and his dad sat with her for a time, including her in their conversation. She stared through them usually, but occasionally she'd act as if she understood what they were saying. Brian had given up on thinking she'd ever know them again. Trying to make conversation with her was painful.

When his phone rang, he was relieved to have an excuse to leave the room. He motioned to his dad who nodded his assent.

Brian took Liz's call in the hallway.

"Now, don't go getting upset or anything 'cause there's nothing you can do. Karen was in an accident and they've taken her to the hospital."

No matter what Liz said, Brian was upset from top to bottom. His heart beat faster and faster until he was light headed. He searched for a place to sit. He'd spent thirty years dreaming about life with Karen and now, if anything happened to her, he didn't know what he'd do.

"How serious is it?"

"I don't know yet. I'm on my way to the hospital now."

"Who found her?"

"Tex. He's the one I'd sent out to check on her before I called you."

"The guy in the wheelchair?"

"Yes. He's so independent, I sometimes forget he's in a chair."

"Then what?"

"He found the bookmobile had rolled over at your place. It was down in a gulley upside down. He couldn't get to her so he called for help. Austin Fire Department was there in minutes and EMS shortly after that."

"Then what?"

"Tex said they got her out and into a stretcher. They had to pull her up by rope. He was close by when the stretcher got to the driveway. He said she didn't look too messed up or anything, but she was unconscious. When he asked, EMS told him she was breathing okay and there were no major wounds, but they couldn't wake her."

CHAPTER EIGHTEEN

Brian flew out of LAX on the last flight of the day going to Austin. While he'd waited for departure, he'd talked to Phil several times to get the latest information about Karen. He wasn't the attending doctor, but Phil knew who to talk to at the hospital. Brian had also talked to Julie more than once since she was with Karen and could give him status reports, too.

He slept fitfully on the three-hour trip that landed at Bergstrom International just before midnight. When he got to the hospital an hour later Julie was in a chair next to Karen's bed. Her eyes were closed and a large opened textbook rested on her chest.

He hardly recognized Karen. There was a clear plastic tube across her face below her nose and a large bandage on the right half of her forehead. But what changed her appearance most was the larger tube in her mouth. She was in a hospital gown and not covered otherwise. Her calves were covered with white plastic that alternately rose and fell with the sound of a motor.

With all the strange things that had happened, he never should have left her alone. Amy could have taken care of his parents in California. He could have postponed his trip until Karen could go with him. Karen wouldn't be in the hospital if he'd been with her. She wouldn't be unconscious if he'd done what men have done since the beginning of time, protected their loved ones from danger.

Julie opened her eyes, looking as if she were coming out of a deep sleep. She caught his eye, smiled softly, and rose. The book fell to the floor with a bang muffled by the sound of the motor under the bed that controlled the airbags on Karen's legs. Julie wrapped her arms around him and held on tightly.

The hug calmed his anger at himself as he realized he wasn't the only one suffering and he shouldn't forget that. He had been in Karen's life briefly compared to Julie, Cathy and many of Karen's other friends. But he loved her just as much.

Julie wore white slacks with a pink polo shirt. Her short hair was combed like her mother's. She pulled out of the embrace and recovered the book she'd dropped on the floor. "I'm glad you're here."

"I just wish I hadn't left her alone."

"You can't be with her all the time. You can't constantly protect her. She's too independent for that. I hope you've learned that about her."

"I know. What about you. Didn't you go to the gulf with your dad?"

"Liz called me on my cell phone and Dad drove me here from Port Aransas. Liz stayed with her until I got here. Cathy's been here, too. She notified Karen's friends. See the flowers?" Julie's voice cracked as she broke into a loud sob.

Brian pulled her close and held her until her shudders subsided.

"I'm sorry," she said, her lower lip quivering. "I haven't had a good cry until now." She pushed away gently, looking into his eyes. "Is she going to be okay?"

He wiped a tear off her cheek with his thumb. "Yes. I talked to Phil by phone several times and he's getting updates from the doctors every time they look at her or when they get a report about her from the staff. He said they did an MRI and didn't find anything life-threatening. Your mom doesn't have a blood clot. Phil said the doctors are confident she'll wake up soon and recover fully."

"But no one knows for sure, do they?"

Brian shook his head slowly as he looked into her eyes, knowing she could see fear in his face. "I trust Phil and I'm confident in the medical reports, but we also need to pray."

Julie turned away from Brian and walked to the window. "Mom is always trying to get me to go back to church. I wish I had. Now if I do it may be too late for her to know. I never told her, but I haven't prayed since I asked God to get Mom and Dad back together so we could be a family again. You know how that turned out. I'm sure it won't do any good for me to pray now."

Brian knew what Julie was going through. He'd been there himself. He also knew there was little he could say that would help. He turned away and focused on Karen. He'd watched her sleep before, but this wasn't the same. He touched her cheek and brushed her hair back. He found a tissue and dabbed at her lips. All the while thinking about what Julie had said about prayer.

"Julie, I went thirty years believing God wouldn't listen to my prayers because of something bad I'd done. It took a long time for me to understand that God always listens." He turned away from Karen and looked at Julie. "Don't do what I did. Don't wait. We don't always get the results we want—like getting your parents together. Sometimes God has a plan we don't know about. In this case, I hope it was to get your mom and me back together."

His admission caused her to grin for the first time since he'd arrived.

"I hadn't thought of that. I know now Mom and Dad get along better since they got divorced. And, it's nice having a dad like you—one I can rely on, but mostly one who loves Mom the way a man should love his wife."

"Thank you. I'm glad to hear that."

Brian felt tears coming on and quickly turned away to look at Karen. "Julie, why don't you take a break since I'm here. Go eat or take a nap. Amy is flying in later today. She'll come sit with me then."

"I could use a shower," Julie said.

"Good. Go take a shower and a nap, too, if you like. Get a good meal. I'll be here and I'll call you if there's any change. Oh, before you go, what do I do?"

She laughed. "Read a book. Or watch TV. Mostly, your job as patient advocate is to make sure she's treated with respect."

"I can do that."

"What if something goes wrong with one of those machines?"

"The nurses are notified automatically, but if they don't show up, go get help."

"Okay. Oh, before you leave I should tell you why your mom wanted you out of town. She'd want me to warn you to be careful."

"It's okay. Dad told me. He wanted me to know everything before he brought me home. I'm staying at his house."

"Good. I told Amy about it, too. We can hire security for you two if you like. What do you think?"

"I don't know. I'll talk to Amy when she gets back and see what she wants to do. I'll probably be here at the hospital most of the time anyway. I can't think about it until Mom is well."

"I understand. I just want you to be safe."

"I'll be careful."

Julie picked up her book and purse and turned to leave. She stopped, looked back at Brian, almost in tears again. "When you pray for her, tell God it's from me, too."

He nodded, holding back his own tears, as she went quickly out the door.

He moved the big chair on the left side of the bed out of the way and knelt with his head on the bed near Karen. The pain in his knees reminded him of when he'd asked her to marry him while they were in the bookmobile parked at the base of Mount Bonnell. He'd placed a book under each knee for padding and that seemed to surprise her more than the fact that he was proposing. But now, here in the hospital on the highly-polished linoleum floor, there was no pain, other than his aching for Karen.

"Dear God..."

He wanted to ask God to heal Karen, but the words eluded him.

He stood, walked around the room. His mind was spinning. There was too much to think about. He'd pray later.

***

He stayed by her side, leaving only long enough to clean up occasionally, and then only if someone he trusted could be with her while he was gone. He ate and slept in her room. She remained the same.

On the third day, he called Richard for the umpteenth time. "Listen. What's being done about catching this Heath guy?"

"We gave the police his name and told them everything we know about him," Richard said. "But we can't say he's the one who caused the accident."

"Accident? Don't call it that. Liz said the police told her the back right wheel was missing. In its place was a jack. The bookmobile was sabotaged." Brian's anger returned.

"Sorry," Richard said. "I know you're upset, but the police are doing all they can."

"Did you tell them about how he followed us in Germany and Belgium? And how he came to the bookmobile?"

"Yes. I told them everything you told me about him."

"Well at least we can get him and his mother to drop the lawsuit now that we've identified him as the culprit."

Richard was silent longer than Brian expected. "Right?" he added, not liking the lack of response from Richard.

"Well," Richard said, "we can try. But since we can't identify him as the person who took the wheel off the bookmobile, there's not much to go on. The other incidents were not criminal."

"What?" Brian asked. "I would think Cloris would want to drop the lawsuit if we agree not to file charges against her son."

"Don't forget the mentality it took to file the case in the first place," Richard said. "She probably isn't threatened by what we know. Or she doesn't care. I'll talk to her lawyer, but don't get your hopes up that this will change anything."

"Well, if that doesn't work, negotiate a settlement. I don't care what it costs. I want this lawsuit out of the way. Karen is going to need to concentrate on healing."

Richard hesitated again. "Brian, I know you mean well, but I can't do that."

"Why?"

"Karen is my client. Not you."

"But I'm her husband and she's unconscious. I'm speaking for her."

"Do you have power of attorney for her?"

"Well, no. We talked about doing that after the honeymoon, but with everything else happening, we haven't done it yet. You know that."

"I'm sorry. That needs to be done."

Brian couldn't believe what he heard. "Talk to Cloris. Get her to drop the suit or I'm coming after her."

"Just calm down, Brian. I can't threaten her and you can't go after her, but I'll try my best to get her to drop the case. In the meantime, I'll postpone the court proceedings due to a medical emergency. What you need to do is forget about everything else and just be there for her. Okay?"

"Thanks, Richard. Sorry for my anger. I know you're doing what's best for Karen." Brian said good bye and disconnected.

He had finally found his prayer voice and periodically he knelt on the floor and leaned into the bed to get as close to her as possible as he talked to God. Today, he did so again. He held his hands in a prayerful grasp at his chest and bowed his head. "Dear God ..."

***

The first thing she saw was the top of a head. No arms, no body, not even a whole head. It could be some man's toupee placed there at a ridiculous odd angle, but reasoning made her think it was more likely someone's head. A familiar head, not often seen at such an angle. She also reasoned she was in bed. It wasn't her bed, though. She looked again and decided the small, round bald spot was the same shape as Brian's. She analyzed the possibilities of such a scene and decided he was on his knees leaning into the bed with his hands together in front of him. He was praying. How nice.

She glanced around and saw a pole next to the bed with lighted equipment and tubes. Beyond Brian's head on her left was a table filled with flowers. She took a deep breath expecting the scent to be pleasant, but it wasn't. She recognized the smell. She was in a hospital.

She didn't want to interrupt Brian's prayers since they were working. She was alive and awake. He'd want to know that. She tried to say his name, but instead squeaked out a muffled sound, not loud enough to be heard over the motor. What motor? The sound of a motor seemed to be connected to her legs. Her calves were covered with white plastic that alternated between small and large. Inflated and deflated. The motor was louder when the bandages got larger. How strange.

She had to let Brian know she was awake. Her left hand was bandaged and connected to tubes. She lifted it anyway, and was surprised it moved. She stared at all the medical stuff on her hand for a few seconds before she gently touched the top of Brian's head. His head popped up with a jerk. Eyes wide open. He smiled. He jumped up and gave her a kiss on the forehead.

"You're awake," he said. "Thank God. You're awake."

She nodded, not sure why she couldn't speak. She opened her mouth and made the squeaky sound again.

"Don't try to talk. They've got a tube down your throat."

She raised her right hand to her mouth, wondering what was wrong with her. There was something in her nose, too. She looked at him pleadingly.

"It's okay. I'm sure they'll take that thing out now that you're awake. I'll call the nurse and see how soon they can remove it." Brian pressed a button on the control hanging on the side of the bed.

"Yes?"

"Mrs. Donelson is awake!"

"I'll tell the doctor." The person on the other end didn't sound as excited as Brian was.

"Any chance you can remove this thing in her mouth so she can talk?" Brian asked.

"I'll check with the doctor, but he may want to see her first."

"Thank you."

Brian smiled. He must have been worried for.... How long? She felt the bookmobile falling over the edge into the gulley and flipping. The fall must have knocked her out. That was Wednesday.

She held her right hand up to her ear with her thumb and little finger out.

"You want to call someone?"

She nodded.

"But you can't talk with that thing in your mouth."

She motioned for him to give her the phone. He handed her his cell phone and she turned it on. It was Saturday. She'd lost three days. She remembered the bookmobile rolling down toward Dry Creek and thanked God she was alive. She handed him the phone.

"What were you doing?" he asked with a smile. "Trying to figure out how long you were out?"

She nodded.

"Do you remember what happened?"

She nodded again.

"You've been unconscious since Wednesday morning. It's now Saturday afternoon. Oh, I guess you know that."

She smiled and nodded.

"I bet you have lots of questions. Do you want to write them down or wait for the doctor to remove that thing?"

She used hand signals to tell him to wait. Her right hand was too bandaged to hold a pencil. She wanted to ask about Julie, though.

It wasn't long before a nurse came in and took her vitals. "Everything looks good," the nurse said. "The doctor gave the okay to remove the endotracheal tube after I check that you're breathing on your own."

Karen nodded.

The nurse determined the frequency of Karen's breath and was apparently satisfied. "Okay, are you ready?"

Karen nodded again, cautiously this time.

The nurse slipped the plastic tubing out slowly and put it in a metal tray on the table next to the bed. "How's that? You may have a sore throat and have trouble talking for a few days. Drink some water if you want to."

"Okay," Karen said with her squeaky voice. "Why did I have that in my throat?" Her voice was raspy.

"I wasn't here when you came in," the nurse said. "But the tube is used to make sure patients can breathe. Since you were in a vehicle accident and were unconscious, they would have inserted it as a precaution."

Brian smiled. "Can she eat something?"

"Not yet. I'll remove the feeding tube, but we'll need to wait for the doctor to change the orders. It shouldn't take long." The nurse paused. "I've got some frozen ice sticks you can suck on. How does that sound?"

Karen nodded. She wasn't hungry, but her mouth was dry. "And something for my lips?"

The nurse left and returned with a popsicle-like treat and a tube of lip balm.

"Did you call Julie?" Karen asked.

"She was here when I got here and she's been in and out every day since. I promised to call her as soon as you woke up. We'll call her in a minute to let her know you're awake."

"Good. First fill in some blanks for me," Karen said. "The last thing I remember is driving off the side of the hill like you said not to do. I couldn't seem to coordinate the clutch, accelerator, parking brake and steering wheel. When I tried to drive out, I must have turned the wrong way and caused the bookmobile to go off the driveway."

Brian was shaking his head while smiling. "No, you didn't cause the tumble. Someone had removed the right rear wheel."

"What? I didn't notice it when I got in."

"No reason you would. Whoever did it left a jack under the axle to keep the vehicle at normal level. I hope they also left fingerprints. I haven't heard yet."

"That doesn't make sense. There wasn't enough room on the right side of the bookmobile for anyone to take off the wheel."

"I thought that, too," Brian said. "But, after looking at the area more closely, I can see how they did it. There is an immediate drop off, but at the point where the back wheel is, there is room to stand and reach the lug nuts."

"Do you know who did it?"

"No. Of course I suspect Heath or his friends. Richard called the police right away and told them everything we know about him. And Liz talked to her friend the police chief to make sure something gets done. I wouldn't be surprised if she also had the Vengeance Squad keeping an eye on Heath as well."

"I'm not sure Heath would do anything to hurt me," she said.

"Maybe not, but we have to let the police look into it. Besides, it might cause Cloris and him to drop the lawsuit."

"I still want to find out why they're doing this."

"I thought you'd want to get the case dropped after this incident."

She shrugged. "I'd love to forget it ever happened. But I can't. The more I've prayed about it the more I need to see it to a conclusion. There's a reason I was sued. A reason we don't know yet."

"A God thing."

"Perhaps."

Brian stared at her long enough for his expression to turn from inconceivability to understanding.

"How else will I ever know why Heath has done what he has done?" she asked.

Brian held her hands in his. "I'll support whatever you want to do. If it was me, I could walk away and never think about why crazy people do crazy things. But we're different that way, and deep down I know your way is best. It's also one of the many reasons I love you."

She pulled him in for a kiss, wondering when she'd last brushed her teeth.

"But I don't think we should stop the police investigation," he said.

"I know. If Heath is arrested and found guilty of tampering with the bookmobile, he'll have to pay the consequences." Karen thought about the accident and shook as she remembered the slow tumble down the ravine. "How bad is the damage?"

"To the bookmobile?" Brian turned and walked to the window before turning back toward Karen. "Not too bad, considering. At least you didn't get into the creek. There were too many trees near the bottom of the cliff for the vehicle to fall in. Ron's taking care of it. I haven't seen it yet. He said it's scratched up pretty bad. It'll need a new paint job. Also, he said the inside looks like all the books were shuffled together."

"Who found me?"

"When you didn't show up at the library and didn't answer your phone, Liz sent Tex out to the house."

"Tex? Isn't he the guy in the wheelchair who wears that ten-gallon hat all the time, even inside the library?"

"That's the one."

"How did he get to me?"

"He didn't, actually. But he discovered where the bookmobile was and called 911. He was there when they brought you up in a stretcher."

Karen smiled, thinking how lucky she was to have so many good friends. "Oh," she said, "I forgot to ask about your mother."

"She's as fine as can be. I left soon after we checked her in, but Amy was in town and was going to drive Dad home."

"That's good. Did you think to tell Julie and Amy to be careful?"

"Yes, but Steve had told Julie already. I talked to Amy about it."

"Is Amy here?"

"She was, but she had to go back to California."

Cathy's shrill laughter filled the entryway. "She's awake? Praise the Lord." She moved quickly to the bed and kissed Karen on each cheek before wiping her own cheeks because of the tears. She hugged Brian. "Thank God," she said.

Cathy was a tall, thin, gray-mopped blur as she sped across the room. Karen loved her best friend even if she never knew what she might say.

"Oh! You got that thing out of your mouth. Finally. I told them you didn't need it. I said you were just taking a nap and you'd be right as rain in no time." Cathy talked so fast, Karen could hardly keep up with her. "Know what? EMS said that seat belt saved your life. Imagine that. You're the only person I know who wears a seatbelt while in her own driveway. I usually don't get mine snapped until I'm at least a block or so from the house. Not anymore, though. Yours saved your life. Police said the bookmobile must have made four and a half turns. You were upside down in there hanging by the belts. Did you know that?"

Cathy didn't wait for an answer. "Don't know why you were unconscious, though. Probably hit your head on something along the way. But it could have been a whole lot worse without that seat belt. You had books all around you, too. I talked to this really cute firefighter who told me they didn't know you were in there until they moved a bunch of books. Are you okay? You haven't said a word."

CHAPTER NINETEEN

For the next two days, Brian and Karen were together around the clock in the hospital room. It reminded him of the time they'd spent in Bruges. No place they had to be. No obligations. Friends came by and visited and, through it all, they grew closer to each other and to their girls. But hidden below the surface was the lawsuit. It hadn't gone away. It was on hold. Richard hadn't been able to get the case thrown out since the police couldn't show Heath or Cloris were involved in any of the incidents involving Karen and Brian.

But the time at Austin General was a reprieve of sorts. Karen didn't mention the case again after that day she regained consciousness, and Brian didn't, either. She did get him to tell her about everything else in the world that happened while she was out of it. Of course, he didn't know much since he'd spent that time with her in the hospital. The expert on world events, and the one who finally told them what had occurred, according to TV news, was Dudley. As it turned out, they hadn't missed much.

Brian and Karen did fun things to pass the time and vowed they'd keep at it when they got home. Someone brought a jigsaw puzzle so big it just barely fit on the hospital table. They had to eat three meals without the space before they finished the puzzle. A nurse brought them a box of dominoes she said she borrowed from the ICU waiting room on the next floor, but neither one of them knew how to play. Julie brought in a game of Scrabble and that is what caught their interest the most. Karen won nearly every game because she used the squares that afforded extra points more than he did. Brian came up with the most unusual words, though. His favorite word during their hospital stay was *oeuvre*. He liked it because it had so many vowels.

Brian and Karen were together when the doctor said she could go home.

"We probably kept you here longer than necessary," Dr. Martin said. "But from the description of the accident, I wanted to make sure you had no internal damage."

A sense of relief engulfed Brian. "And you haven't found anything, have you?" he asked.

"No. She's perfect."

"She sure is," Brian said, leaning in for a kiss.

Karen pushed him away, lovingly, and smiled. "I'm ready to go, Doc. I need to get this guy out of here soon. He hasn't had a shower in days and I no longer recognize him with that beard."

Brian stroked his chin. It wasn't exactly a beard, but it was a start. The last time he shaved was the day he took his mother to the facility. He counted on his fingers. Five days. At first he didn't have time to shave, but once Karen said she liked his facial hair he decided to keep it.

After the doctor left, Brian got that kiss he'd clowned about. She pulled him back for a second one and held him close. "I was kidding," she said.

"I know. I can tell by the kiss."

Julie was in and out several times each day, taking turns with Brian so that someone would be with her around the clock. When the doctor announced Karen could check out, Julie was at Steve's house.

Karen sat up on the edge of the bed. "Okay. Time to pack."

Besides the flowers, there wasn't much in the room that didn't stay. Julie had brought in some clothes for Karen to wear home. She put them on and put the remaining personal items into the plastic bag the clean clothes had been in.

All they had to do now was wait for the nurse to bring the discharge papers.

"Don't you need to get back to work?" Karen asked.

"Me? What about you? I'm not going to work until you do."

"Do we have a job? Is the bookmobile operable?"

"Well," he said, "sort of."

"What does that mean?"

He laughed. "It means the engine works and the wheels seem to go in the right direction, generally, but it's a mess."

"Is that all?"

"Oh, and there are a few broken windows."

"A few?" she asked.

"Yes. Well, by that I mean all."

"So we can't go to work yet."

"No, but it won't be long."

Brian's cell rang. He looked at the screen and smiled. "It's Amy." He clicked the answer button and the speaker button so Karen could hear. "Hi, sweetie. How are things in California?"

"Hi, Daddy. Not so good." Her voice was too solemn. Brian frowned.

"Is it Mom?" he asked.

"No. It's Grandpa."

"Grandpa?" Brian flinched as he waited for the bad news. Karen's comforting hands closed around his free one.

"We're not sure of the details yet. He's had some type of heart incident. Grandma's special care nurse was at the house picking up her things when he suddenly passed out. She called 911 and stayed with him until they got there. Afterwards she called to tell me where they took him. He was alive she said, but we think he had a stroke."

"So, you haven't talked to the doctor yet?" Brian asked.

"No. I'm on my way to the hospital now. I'll call back when I know something."

"Thank you," Brian's voice cracked as he spoke.

"Dad, I've got it. You stay close to Karen. I'll call you when I know something."

"Okay. Yes. I appreciate that. I'll stay with Karen."

"How's she doing?" Amy asked.

Karen grabbed the phone. "I'm doing great. Going home today. Your dad can leave here if need be. Call us back after you talk to the doctor, okay?"

"Will do. It's great to hear you're heading home today."

Karen handed the phone to Brian.

"Amy, take care and call soon. Love you."

Brian pressed the off button and pulled Karen into his arms.

"You should make flight arrangements as soon as possible," Karen said.

"I'm not leaving you again. I don't care what happens outside our world together. Nothing is more important than being with you. Until that crazy kid is arrested and put away, I'm not going to leave your side."

"Yes you are," she said.

"Huh?"

"If your father has had a stroke or a heart attack or whatever it is, you're going to California to be with him. You have to."

"But—"

"No buts."

"Amy said she'd be with him. She said I should stay with you. I'm not going to leave you at home alone again. That's it. End of discussion."

She paused. "Okay. What if I go stay at Cathy's until you get back?"

"I'm not going anywhere."

"You're going to be with your father. He could die. He's probably been holding onto life until he knew your mother was taken care of. How'd he look when you saw him last?"

Brian remembered the day he and his dad drove his mother to the care center. "Not good. But he wasn't dying. Sure, Mom's illness was rough on him, but now is his time to recover. The stress is off and he can live a happier life. I think he'll be okay in a few days. I'm staying here with you."

"You can't be sure of that. Wait and see what the doctor says. If you need to go, I wouldn't want you not to because of me. Understand?"

He fought the urge to forget everything and stay with her. "Yes. I think I do." And he did understand, finally.

***

Karen sat on the edge of the hospital bed, dressed and waiting for the nurse to bring her discharge papers. Brian was silent. She didn't know what else to say to him, and knew he was torn about what to do. He was staring at the floor when his phone rang again. On the third ring, he straightened his back and glanced at Karen. She nodded, sure of the message.

By the time he hung up, he was back to his old self. He turned to Karen. "The doctor told Amy I should go see Dad right away."

"Then you must go. I'll stay at Cathy and Dudley's and I promise to stay out of trouble." She tried to be funny but he was in no mood for humor. "With Dudley as a bodyguard, no one would dare get near me."

"Are you sure you want me to go?" he asked.

She got up and hugged him. "Yes. I'll miss you, but I'll be okay. What happened to me with the bookmobile was not your fault."

He shook his head. "I'm worried about Dad, but I can't bear leaving you again after what happened."

"I know, but you can't always protect me. I must be able to care for myself." She hugged him again. "Now, go. I'll call Cathy as soon as you leave."

"Call her now," he said.

"What? You don't trust me?"

"No, no, it's not that. I just want to make sure she's available."

Karen picked up her phone and punched the "Cathy" button.

"Hello," Cathy said. "Need me to bring something to the hospital?"

"Yes," Karen said. "Bring me a ride. Can I stay with you and Dudley a few days?"

"Sure. What's up? Where's Brian?" Cathy asked.

"He's here now, but his daughter called to say his dad had a possible stroke and the doctor thinks Brian should return to California right away."

"Oh, I'm sorry. Bet he's torn about what to do."

Karen looked at Brian and smiled. "Yes, he won't leave until he knows I can stay with you."

"Well, tell him good bye. You can always stay with me. When are you getting out of that place?"

"Right now. You ready for company?"

"All right. I'm on my way."

Karen punched the off button. "She's on her way."

"You're positive I should go?" Brian asked.

She hugged him hard and held him tight. "I'll be fine. You have to go. It's family. I'll call Kay to let the Combine know what happened. I'd go with you, but I'm not ready to travel that far yet. We'll talk whenever we want."

"Okay," he said. "I'm going to miss you."

After Brian kissed her and left, Karen realized she wasn't as well as she wanted to be. Not because of Brian leaving. She was honest with him about that. What she didn't tell him and didn't understand was how much Heath's involvement in everything was bothering her. She'd based her decision to fight the lawsuit on her belief it was God's will. She'd believed that could help the young man, as well as let the world know she was innocent. But if he was the one who put her in the hospital, perhaps she'd misunderstood what she was supposed to do. Surely God wouldn't want her to put herself and her family in danger. It might be time to settle, to put an end to the confrontation. Maybe all they wanted was money. Maybe God didn't care one way or the other.

Doubt about God's presence, even existence, came over her for the first time in her adult life, causing tears to flow. Karen didn't want anyone to see her in this state of confusion. She went into the bathroom and shut the door. She pressed against the closed door and prayed. She said the words that always brought her comfort, but nothing happened. Shocked, she tried again. Nothing. She said the Lord's Prayer over and over again. Finally, she felt normal. That was when she noticed she was kneeling on the hard tile floor. She laughed aloud when she realized God was back. God hadn't left her.

"Karen?" A voice came from behind the closed door. "Are you okay?"

"Yes. I'll be out in a minute." She stood, washed her hands and opened the door. Richard stood alone in the room.

"Hi. I was just cleaning up. Getting ready to go home."

"Where's Brian?" Richard asked.

"He just left. His father is in the hospital. Brian's gone back to California."

"Oh? How's he doing?"

"It was a stroke, but we're not sure how serious it is."

"Tell Brian we're praying for the best. Do you need a ride?" Richard asked.

"No. Thanks. Cathy's on her way to pick me up. Brian insisted I stay with her until he gets back. He worries about me so much, you know."

"Yes. I understand. I wanted to let you know the plaintiffs dropped the case against Brian as soon as I threatened to file the Rule 13."

"That's good to hear. Did you tell Brian?"

"Not yet, but I will. The main reason I came to see you is to see if you would consider mediation. The judge recommended it and the plaintiff has agreed. I think it's a good idea."

"Mediation? That sounds like settling." Karen put her purse on the bed next to the plastic bag containing her dirty clothes.

"Mediation is different. What we would do is go to the office of a certified mediator. The plaintiffs and the defendant go into different rooms and never meet face to face. They'll describe in writing what they want and then you can make a counter offer."

"Sounds like agreeing to settle to me." Karen said.

"Well, you can think of it that way if you like, but it's a good way of going back and forth with offers and counteroffers in a short period of time without the constraints of the court. The mediator talks to each party, one at a time, and keeps the process moving toward resolution. Based on our history with the plaintiffs I can't be sure they're serious or if this is just another delaying tactic. However, since they have to pay the mediator the same amount you do, I think they're serious about reaching an agreement outside of court."

Karen wasn't sure what to do. She'd prayed for guidance when Richard showed up. Perhaps this was the answer to her prayer. "How long does mediation take?" she asked.

"Can't say. If they're serious about ending this case, we could be through in one day. More likely, we'll be there a week."

Karen paused. "What do you think I should do?"

"I recommend mediation because of this particular case. There's a good chance you can put an end to the litigation by doing so. If it doesn't work, all you've lost is some time, and, of course, some more money."

"Okay. Let's do it."

"Good." Richard said. "I'll call them and take the next available appointment with a mediator. Sure you don't need a ride home?"

Cathy walked in. "Your car awaits, madam."

CHAPTER TWENTY

After the first day of mediation, Karen was ready to give up on the approach because of the plaintiff's unreasonable demands. Cloris's first offer asked for two million dollars plus every gift Karen had received from Ernest during their marriage. By the end of the day Cloris had lowered the amount requested to a mere million dollars plus all gifts from Ernest.

Karen couldn't think of a single gift she'd received from Ernest, much less one of any value. Richard said they were probably just fishing to see what they could find. Cloris and Heath had yet to be deposed and, as long as the mediation continued, they wouldn't have to be. Karen wondered if it was all a ploy just to continue their harassment. When Karen said they give up on mediation and go back to court, Richard suggested she should give it more time.

Richard wasn't as disappointed with their progress in mediation as Karen was. He said that often happens the first day. He was sure the plaintiffs would be more reasonable tomorrow.

The second day of mediation began the same unproductive way so Karen decided to see if she couldn't move things along.

"Richard, I want to talk to Heath alone. Can you set that up?"

"What? I don't know. That's not usually done."

"Tell them I won't consider more offers until I talk to Heath. And make sure they understand he and I meet alone and off the record."

"Well, I can try. All they can do is say no."

Richard called Sam Olsen, the mediator, to the room assigned to Karen. Olsen was a man in his fifties, overweight, but he came across as a professional, more like a judge in Karen's mind than a lawyer. She'd seen the certificates on the walls showing he'd been a mediator for eighteen years. The three of them sat around the table.

"Sam," Richard said, "Karen wants to talk to Heath."

Sam studied Karen before turning his gaze to Richard. "I don't recommend meetings between parties. That's why we have these separate rooms and make a special effort to keep you separated at lunch and when coming and going. Getting the parties together invalidates the whole purpose of using a mediator."

"We understand," Richard said. "But, as you can see, we're not progressing anyway. Why not try something different since Karen is willing."

She reached over and put her hand on Sam's arm. "I don't want to mess up the process. I want to know what Heath is thinking. What he wants from me. That's all. His mother and their attorney haven't provided any explanation. We never had a chance to depose him because of their delaying tactics. His mother has attacked me criminally and should be in jail, or at least counseling. I've never had a chance to even meet Heath, although he followed Brian, my husband, and me to Europe and back. I don't want to negotiate the case with him. I just want to get to know him."

Sam pushed back from the table, crossed his arms and was silent for several seconds. Finally, he nodded. "You just want to talk to the young man? Not negotiate the case with him?"

Karen nodded.

"Okay. This is highly unusual, but I'll talk to the attorney and we'll see what happens."

Sam returned about ten minutes later. "You get to meet with Heath alone."

Karen smiled.

"Any conditions?" Richard asked.

"Not really," Sam said. "I presented them with the request and Karen's reason for it. I let them talk it over while I was out of the room. It wasn't long before they called me back in and said okay."

There was a knock on the door. When Sam opened the door, Heath looked in. He paused momentarily before he moved awkwardly into the room, appearing younger than twenty-two.

"Sit here," Sam said, pointing to the chair across from Karen. "We'll leave you two alone."

Sam nodded at Richard and they walked out of the room, shutting the door behind them.

As soon as they were alone, Karen waited while Heath looked around.

"Your room is like ours," he said. "Mother doesn't like the room we're in. I don't know why. It's the same as this. She said you probably got the best room."

Karen glanced around, noticing the room for the first time. It was plain, but clean. There were a few decorator prints on the wall and a healthy-looking ivy twisted out of a large blue ceramic vase on a corner table. "Yes," she said, "it is a nice room."

He took the seat Sam had pointed out and folded his hands.

"I'm glad to officially meet you, Heath."

"Me too. I'm sorry I scared you," he said, quickly looking down.

"Scared me?"

"You know. That day I visited the bookmobile."

"Oh, that," she said. "My husband was angry, not me. You didn't scare me. In fact I wanted to talk to you."

He looked surprised.

"Now that we're alone, I'm not sure what to say."
She watched him to see how he would react. His face
was blank. "My friend Cathy always tells me to pray
for guidance when I don't know what to do. Would
you mind if we pray first?"

Heath shrugged.

She bowed her head. "Dear God, help us as we meet
and talk. Guide us and show us the way to resolve
differences." When she looked up she saw Heath
staring at her with his arms across his chest.

"My mother says religion is all a bunch of hooey.
She said Ernest was a hypocrite. Said you're all
hypocrites."

Karen waited a few seconds, digesting Heath's
comment before continuing. She said a silent prayer for
him, asking God's special care for this young man.

"Heath, do you hate me?"

He cocked his head and narrowed his eyes as if
trying to determine if he did or not. "No. I don't think I
do."

"Then you didn't mean to hurt me when you took
the wheel off the bookmobile?"

"I didn't do that." His voice was stronger.

She smiled. She believed him and was glad it wasn't
him. She wondered why it mattered.

"Heath, what do you want from me?"

He scratched his head, leaned back and sat up
straight in his chair before leaning in slightly toward
her. "I want to know more about Ernest. I mean, my
father."

If she'd tried, she never would have guessed that was what he would say. "Did you ask your mother?"

"I did, but I'm not sure I can trust her when it comes to Ernest. She says he was a terrible man who didn't love me. You must have loved him to stay with him the way you did when he died. I'd like to hear about him from you."

Karen smiled, relieved. "Yes, I loved him. He was a good man who made a mistake, but he would never hurt anyone on purpose."

Heath leaned over the table on his elbows, getting as close to Karen as the table between them allowed. "See. That's what I mean. What else can you tell me?"

"Heath, why didn't you call and ask me about your father? Why sue me?"

He cocked his head again, as if looking for the answer. "I was going to write you an e-mail, but when I asked Mother, she told me that wouldn't work because you're so mean. She said you wouldn't care about me. Besides, Mother wanted you to pay for what you did to her."

Karen couldn't think of anything she'd done to Cloris, but didn't want to bring that up and change the direction of the conversation with Heath. If all he wanted was to talk about Ernest, she could do that.

A comfort she sometimes felt during her morning devotions gushed into her body. An image of a frail, dying Ernest handing her all his earthly possessions in a shoebox. She heard his cracking voice and saw his bloodshot eyes. He beseeched her to give the box to his son. It contained a few knickknacks and trinkets. Was that all Heath needed from his father? She had to find that box.

"Heath, I have something from your father that he wanted me to give you. I'll try to find it tonight and bring it tomorrow. I can tell you more about your father then. I promise. I'll look for some pictures, too. Can we meet alone again?"

"Yes. Uncle Hank and Mother said I couldn't talk to you today. But since I'm of age, I insisted. Now I'm glad I did." He smiled for the first time.

There was a spark in his face she hadn't seen before. The promise of a memory from his father was important to him. She hoped she could deliver.

***

Karen had been out of the hospital for a week, and she had no aches and pains, no dizziness at all. Even so, the doctor had told her not to drive for a couple of more weeks as a precaution. As Richard took her back to Cathy and Dudley's house she thought about how to get to the Sunset Valley house to search for the shoebox and the mementoes she'd promised Heath. Cathy could drive her.

After dinner, she told Cathy about her meeting with Heath and how she'd promised him something from his father. "I've got to find that box. Will you take me over to the house and help look?"

"Sure," Cathy said. "Let's put these dishes in the dishwasher and change into some casual clothes first."

"Thank you. I know deep down this is important. Remember when I told you God wanted me to go through this lawsuit for a reason? I think this is it. It's so simple. Well, if we can find the box, it will be."

When the dishwasher was started and they'd changed clothes, they grabbed their purses and headed out.

"Bye, Dudley," Cathy hollered. "Karen and I are going over to her house. Be back in a few minutes."

***

Cathy parked in front of the garage, but before she could turn off the engine, Karen grabbed her hand.

"I don't want to scare you," Karen said, "but I think someone followed us here."

Cathy glanced out the door. "Huh? I didn't see anyone."

"I might be paranoid after everything that's happened, but a black pickup, just like the one that followed me before, turned onto Sunset Trail behind us. It slowed and kept going after we pulled in here."

"Are you sure it's the same one? Pickups are common in this town. Lots of black ones, too. Probably someone who lives here."

"I don't think so. I haven't been gone that long. I know every vehicle for the fourteen homes on the street. No black pickups." She turned to Cathy. "I'll understand if you'd rather leave. I don't want to put you in a dangerous situation."

"Nah," Cathy said. "Let's do this. But let's hurry. Just in case."

"Thanks." Karen said. "I'd sure like to find that box tonight. Oh, piffle. I left my garage door opener in my car at home. Leave your lights on while I punch in the code."

She got out of the car and used the keypad on the side of the garage to open the door. When the door rose all the way, she went in and turned on the lights. Cathy turned off the engine and joined her in the garage.

They went in and searched the entire house. Closets, cabinets, nooks and crannies. Nothing. Karen was about to give up.

"Hey!" Cathy snapped her fingers. "What about that storage area above the garage?"

"Oh, yeah. I put stuff up there we never used," Karen said.

"That must be where the shoebox is. Let's go."

When they got back to the garage, Karen found the rope connected to the attic ladder. It creaked as she pulled it down. When she could reach the ladder she unfolded it until it touched the concrete garage floor. "Okay," Karen said, "let's see what we find."

She started up the steps. Halfway into the attic storage room, she found the light switch on the rafter near the opening. A yellowish glow from a low wattage bulb illuminated the area. She climbed the rest of the way onto the plywood floor. There was barely room to stand in the center where the roof peaked. The attic held the heat from the sun beating down on the roof all day making it hot and stuffy. The storage area was dusty and as Karen stood cobwebs tickled her face. She quickly scanned the area for the shoebox, hoping she wouldn't have to stay up there long. This was her last hope to find Ernest's treasures, what little there were.

The attic door slammed shut with a bang causing Karen to jump and turn toward the noise. Cathy had followed and stood between Karen and the attic door. Dust rose from where the opening had been.

Karen stared at the attic door with the folded ladder. "Why'd you do that?" Karen asked.

Cathy's eyes were wide. "Do what?"

"Why'd you fold up the ladder and shut the door?"

"I didn't. I was right here when it closed by itself."

Karen walked to the ladder, now flattened and in the attic area with them. "Well, maybe the spring lock is broken. We'll have to push it down. Shouldn't be hard to do. Might as well find what we came up here for first. No use opening this thing and have it spring up again."

"Okay," Cathy said. "I'll start looking on this side and you start there. Yuck. There are cobwebs everywhere. Yuck, yuck, yuck."

Karen shook her head and started looking around for the box.

It didn't take long. When she saw the dust-covered shoebox, it all came back to her.

In her memory, Ernest's instructions had been clear. In his weak voice, she heard him again as he'd asked her to give the box to Heath when he was old enough to understand. He'd made her promise. She caught her breath. The memory of Ernest's rapidly weakening health pained her. And her failure to carry out a dying man's request was unforgivable. She had forgotten. She had failed Ernest and Heath. She had failed God. It was all her fault. The lawsuit was her fault.

The good news was she'd found the shoebox. She had something to give to Heath tomorrow.

CHAPTER TWENTY-ONE

Brian looked at his watch again. It was eight o'clock, ten o'clock in Austin, and he couldn't reach Karen. He'd called a dozen times and she hadn't called back yet. He was at the hospital and had to go to the waiting room every time he made a call so he wouldn't disturb his dad. He called Cathy's number, too, but she hadn't answered, either. Finally, he found Cathy's home phone and tried it.

"Hello," a man's voice said.

"Dudley? Is that you?"

"Yes. Who's this?"

"It's Brian Donelson. I'm trying to reach Karen. Is she there?"

"No. She was here, though. I think she's sleeping here again tonight. But she's not here now."

"Do you happen to know where she is? She's not answering her cell phone."

"Nope. I'm not sure where they went. All I remember is Cathy said they were going someplace and they'd be back in a few minutes."

"When was that?"

"I don't know for sure when they left. I was watching TV. Earlier they were talking about going to Karen's house. Maybe they went there. Yeah, I think that's where they went."

It would take ten or fifteen minutes to drive from Cathy's house to Karen's, so that could be why they'd said they'd be back in a few minutes. "Would you tell Karen to call me when she gets back?" Brian asked, hoping he was wrong about them returning to the place where Karen had gotten the threatening phone call.

"Sure will. Is that all? My show's on. Bye." Dudley hung up.

Dudley wasn't as reliable as Brian would have liked. He lived in a world of his own, seemingly unaware of time or surroundings. No telling when the girls had left. He wouldn't count on Dudley to pass a message to Karen. Something could be wrong and Dudley wouldn't know it if it hit him in the face.

He called the Sunset Valley land line and let it ring ten times before giving up.

He considered calling Phil and asking him to get the Combine out to find her, but he knew someone with better resources for this situation. He dialed the number.

"Hello, Brian. How's your dad?"

"Hi, Liz. Sorry to call you this late. He's doing better, but I can't leave here yet."

"Praise the Lord," Liz said.

"Listen, I need some help."

"Tell me. I'll take care of it."

Liz was a person he could count on. If she said she'd take care of it, she would. "I'm worried about Karen. I think she and Cathy went to Karen's house in Sunset Valley. Now neither one is answering their phones. I also tried the house phone. Maybe they left their cell phones at Cathy's or something, but with all that's happened lately, I'd feel better if Karen would tell me she's okay. Can you help?"

"Sure. From what you've told me I don't think I'll call the police, but I know a couple of guys who love to get involved in situations like this."

"You're talking about Chris and Tex, the Vengeance Squad?" Brian asked.

"Right. I don't know how they got that name of Vengeance Squad. They're such sweet boys. Anyway, don't worry. I'll get them to go to the house. If Karen and Cathy are there, we'll get Karen to call you. If they're not there, I'll let you know that, too. And we'll get a search started."

"Thanks, Liz. There's probably a simple explanation. Either way, I appreciate you doing this."

***

"I found it," Karen said, as she held back tears.

"Good," Cathy said. "Now, let's get out of here. It's hot and yucky in this attic."

Karen blew the dust off the old shoebox and, resisting an urge to look inside, went to the attic door to open it so they could climb down and go home.

Cathy was sneezing non-stop now from the dust and, knowing her friend the way she did, Karen suspected Cathy would be complaining about claustrophobia next. Karen placed the box beside the ladder door and gently pushed down on it with one foot to see if that would release the spring. The door moved away from the ceiling of the garage slightly, but when it did, dark gray smoke floated in. Karen quickly lifted her foot off the attic door.

"Hey! What's that? I got a whiff of smoke!" Cathy hollered, followed by a loud sneeze. "Smell that?"

Something was seriously wrong. Karen's skin crawled as she accepted the possibility that they could be trapped with a fire below them. Several causes came to mind and none of them were good. "Yes," she said. "I not only smelled it. I saw it and felt the heat."

Cathy pushed on Karen as if she wanted to go past her and push the ladder door down. "There's a fire in the garage. We've got to get out of here. Fast!"

"Calm down," Karen said. "That door is keeping the fire and smoke out of the attic. We don't want to go down where the fire is."

Cathy turned her head one way and then the other. "But we have to. There's no other way out of here."

Karen touched her pants pocket. "Did you bring your phone?" she asked.

Cathy held out both hands. "No. Did you?"

"Mine's in my purse in the car."

"Mine too," Cathy said. "We can't call for help. We're going to die here, aren't we?" She sneezed loudly and moved closer to the attic entrance.

Karen reached over and placed a hand on Cathy's shoulder. "Not if I can help it. Let me think." Karen paused for a few seconds, holding on to her friend, afraid she might try to open the door blocking the fire. "There's another way out of here. Remember the attic access door in Julie's bedroom?"

"But this storage area is walled off. We can't get from here to there." Cathy's voice rose as she became more frazzled.

"We can if we have to." Karen picked up the treasure box and handed it to her. "Hold this while I find a way." She needed to keep Cathy busy so she wouldn't panic and try to climb down to where the fire burned below them.

Cathy took the box and scanned the storage room. Karen was skeptical about their chances of getting through the wall and over to the other exit in the dark before the fire reached them. Still, it was the only way out.

She searched for anything that might help them escape. There was a lamp shade with no lamp, a box of extra tiles from the time she'd had the kitchen redone, and over in one corner was a box of Julie's old toys. She'd saved them for the grandkids she might have one day. It would be sad if they were lost in a fire. There was also a beat-up brown-checkered suitcase and she remembered it had belonged to Ernest. There were more memories in it. When he died, she'd put all his hospital and doctor bills in that suitcase along with what was left of his clothes. Would Heath want such things? She shook her head. Focus! Right now it was more important to get out alive, with or without what they'd come for. But it'd be a shame to leave without something for Heath. She grabbed the suitcase and kept looking for a tool to get them out.

There! Off to one side was an old real estate for-sale sign on a metal stake, left from the time she'd planned to sell the house and move to another school district for Julie. As it turned out, Julie loved her school and her teachers so they stayed where they were. The agent never came back for the sign and Karen eventually moved it to storage.

She carried the suitcase and the sign to the sheetrock wall that separated the storage room from the rest of the house. She set the suitcase next to the wall, held the sign over her shoulder with the pointed end of the metal stake toward the wall and jabbed as hard as she could. The first strike hit a stud and jarred her body as the force of her movement stopped abruptly.

Moving her mental target six inches to the right she struck again, harder than before. The metal tip tore into the wall, causing the white chalky center section to fragment and fall to the attic floor. More chalk dust flew out as she pulled the stake out and struck the wall repeatedly. When the hole was large enough, she used her hands to pull the sheetrock down and away from the two-by-four studs. It wasn't long before Cathy helped, jerking the wall material away as fast as she could with one hand, while not letting go of the box Karen had asked her to hold.

Soon the opening was large enough for them to crawl through on their hands and knees into the unfinished part of the attic.

"Don't step on the ceiling itself," Karen said. If you do you might fall through. Put your weight on the rafters."

"Okay. Yuck. What's this pink stuff. It's all over the place. It's so dark. We'll never make it. I'm going to fall through the ceiling and break my neck. I just know it." Cathy's harsh breathing, punctuated by sneezes and coughing, strengthened Karen's resolve to get them out quickly.

"That's insulation," Karen said. "Here, let me take the box and you can hold on better without getting any on you." Karen took the box from Cathy and put it in the suitcase she pulled behind her. "Come on, Cathy. You can do it. Stay right behind me."

The further they went away from the opening they had made in the sheetrock wall, the darker it got.

Karen hoped Cathy wouldn't panic when it got completely dark. They were halfway across the family room now, but as soon as they turned right toward the bedroom it would be darker. Even so, she wouldn't have any trouble finding the attic door in the dark. She knew exactly where it was. What she didn't know was whether she could get to it before Cathy fell apart from fear.

They reached the turn and Karen stared into the dark cavern that was the attic above the hall and three bedrooms. "Cathy," she said. "It's going to get darker here. I know the way, though. Grab the end of the suitcase and follow me."

"What?" Cathy's voiced squeaked. "Darker? I can barely see now."

"It'll be okay," Karen said. "We're almost there. Hold on and I'll guide you."

The exit wasn't far now and they could easily get there before the fire spread that far. She couldn't tell Cathy, but Karen wondered what they'd find when they got there. Would the arsonist be waiting for them?

As they duck walked toward Julie's bedroom, Karen became concerned because it didn't get as dark as she thought it would. As they got closer to where the opening should be, she knew why. Light shimmered in through the open attic door. That could mean trouble. But they'd come this far and she didn't intend to stop now. If someone out there tried to scare them, or hurt them, they were going to find out it wouldn't be easy.

She wished she had brought the for-sale sign with them. That would scare them.

"Hey," Cathy said. "That attic door is open. That's not good is it?"

"Shh!" she whispered. "We're going to find out." She saw a shadow move and knew someone was there, but she didn't care. At least there were no flames and no smoke. She had to get Cathy down, away from the danger of the fire. She'd deal with the intruders once they were out. She moved the suitcase in front of her and started down the folding ladder, having decided to use the luggage to hit anyone who came toward them.

CHAPTER TWENTY-TWO

What she found was Tex in his wheelchair smiling so big she couldn't help but smile back. Chris stood next to him and offered to take her bag.

"What's happening?" Cathy said from the attic, her voice shaky. "Are you okay?"

"Everything's fine," Karen said. "Come on down."

"Liz called," Tex said, "and told us to check on you. Looks like you didn't need our help."

"What about the fire in the garage?"

"All out," Chris said. "And we got the license number of the truck that sped out of here as we drove in. I tried to block it, but he rammed his way through your neighbor's wooden fence and got away. We used a fire extinguisher and got the fire out before it had time to do much damage. We were going to call the fire department after we found you, but I'll let you decide if that's needed. We called the police about the pickup and the neighbor's fence."

Cathy grabbed Chris and hugged him before she bent down and hugged Tex, too. "Thank you, thank you, thank you."

"Oh, by the way," Chris said to Karen, "call your husband. He's worried about you."

Karen surveyed the damage in the garage and decided not to call the fire department. Tex and Chris had stopped the spread of the flames before they did little more than smolder. The arsonist had used some damp cardboard boxes that failed to catch fire to anything else in the garage.

She was glad the guys had called the police and offered to stay to report the incident, because all she wanted to do was get back to Cathy's house and look at what was in the old brown suitcase and the dusty shoebox she'd put in it.

While Cathy drove, Karen called Brian and told him she'd left her phone in the car while they searched the attic and that they were okay. She quickly changed the subject to tell him how happy she was with what she'd found.

"Well, you didn't lie to him," Cathy said after Karen ended the call, "but don't you think you left out a few of the important details?"

"He'd just worry if I told him about the fire. He has enough on his mind right now."

Karen noticed the smudges on Cathy's face and dust on her clothes, probably a match to her own. It was a good thing Brian was out of town. He'd have a cow if she came home looking the way Cathy looked.

"I'll tell him everything later, when he's able to handle it. Besides, nothing happened. We're okay."

"You might be. What am I going to tell Dudley? We're dirty and smell like smoke. I'll never go in an attic again. That was scary stuff. You do realize what could have happened to us up there, don't you?"

"Yes," Karen said. "But it didn't."

At first, Karen was angry with herself for failing to carry out Ernest's wishes. But it happened so long ago, and she didn't think the trinkets were important. She didn't know what she could have done differently. Besides, a sane person would have asked her about Ernest, not sued her. That would have reminded her about the shoebox without all the hassle of a courtroom battle. Even though her clothes were dirty and she had attic dust and insulation in her hair and her legs hurt from duck walking, she was surrounded by the peace she felt every time a prayer was answered.

They met in the kitchen after Cathy checked on Dudley. Neither of them wanted to change clothes before they examined the loot, so they sat on the tiled floor to keep from soiling the furniture or carpet and opened the shoebox. Karen was anxious to see what was there.

"Dudley is already in bed," Cathy said. "Watching TV. He didn't even notice my messy clothes and hair. But he did remember to tell me Brian called."

"That's pretty good for Dudley. Cathy, I want to thank you for remembering where the shoebox was stored and for helping me retrieve it. I couldn't have done it without you."

"It was an adventure I'll never forget," Cathy said, brushing insulation off her pants.

Karen reached into the old box and pulled out the letters on top of the trinkets. She grabbed the crinkled rubber band that had long since lost its elasticity. It had held the letters together for decades, but now, after doing its job for so long it crumbled in her hands and fell to the floor. She read the writing on the outside of each envelope and cried. She passed the stack of old letters to Cathy and bent over, holding her head in her hands as the tears leaked through her palms.

"My God, my God. What have I done?" She now understood Ernest. She could let go of her anger for mistakes made during that part of her life. She married him to provide him life insurance and ease the final days of his life, but she'd loved him, too. He'd tried to be a good father. It was up to her to make amends for him with his son.

***

The next day at the mediator's office Karen once again asked for a private meeting with Heath. He entered the room slowly, his eyes locked on the old brown checkered suitcase. He went to the chair across from Karen where he had sat the day before.

"Come over here and sit next to me," Karen said. "I have some things I want to show you. To give you."

She watched him as he slowly moved around the table and sat down. She couldn't tell if he was happy or frightened or both. The look on his face was one of awe.

When he was seated, he turned to her as if letting her know he was ready. She opened the shoebox first, took out the stack of letters held together by a fresh rubber band and placed them in his hands. He held them as if they were fine crystal or a fragile flower. A smile slowly grew on his face, but he didn't open the letters. Instead, he leaned over the table to see what else was in the box. Karen opened the suitcase and placed the stack of hospital bills and clothing on the table alongside the shoebox. His eyes darted from one to the other before he focused on Karen. "Is this really from my dad?" he asked.

"Yes," Karen said. "It'll take hours to read it all, but look at the notation on each envelope." She took the stack of letters out of his hands, gently, not wanting to alarm him. "This one was to be read to you on your first birthday, or read by you when you were old enough." She opened the letter and unfolded it.

Dear Son,

I'm sorry I can't be with you on this special day, but I want you to know how much I love you. I don't know if your mother told you or not, but the only reason I'm not with you on your birthday is because I am very ill. I have a cancer that is not treatable. My regret is that I won't see you grow up and become a man. I love you and wish you a happy birthday.

Love, Dad

When she looked up, she saw a tear making its way slowly down Heath's cheek.

She patted his hand. "All of these letters were written by your father for you. There's one for each birthday up to your eighteenth. There are also Christmas cards and some letters that weren't for any particular occasion. I didn't read them all, just enough to determine what they are. I'm sorry I didn't get them to you sooner. All I can say is that I put them away for so long I forgot they were there. I know that's not a good excuse, but that's what happened."

He took the stack of envelopes and turned them around, looking at them from every angle.

She continued explaining. "I didn't know what was in this box when I put it away for safekeeping. If I had, I would have made more of an effort to see that you got them sooner. I was upset by your father's death and didn't want to think about it more than I had to. Can you forgive me?"

He sat the stack of envelopes down gingerly. "Yes, I can. I do. Can you forgive me and my Mother for suing you?"

"Yes, of course. I'm just sorry it took legal action to get my attention."

"Me too. What else is in there?" he asked, looking at the old shoebox.

"Let's see," she said, pulling it toward them. "The bottom of the box is covered with a variety of lapel pens. Probably places your father worked or supported." She picked up a ribbon with a medal hanging on it. "Here is an award he got."

"That's a good conduct medal," Heath. "He must've been a soldier."

Karen remembered the military veterans' wall at church and how she'd noticed his photo there soon after she'd met him. The black and white photo showed a younger Ernest in his dress uniform. That picture still hung there after decades. She'd get a copy made for Heath.

"Yes, he was." She dug around in the box and found a card showing he'd been honorably discharged from the army, along with several other medals. "Yes. Look at these."

Heath took the card, read it and smiled. "He was in the army. I wonder what these other medals are for."

"I'm not sure, but I bet you can find out."

"Yeah," he said. "I can look them up on the Internet."

Karen took out another card. "Here's one that says he donated ten gallons of blood."

"Wow," said Heath. "That's a lot."

"Sure is. Your father was a good man."

Heath frowned. "Mother said he wasn't. She said he didn't care about me and never tried to see me after they were divorced."

"That's not true," Karen said as she reached into the suitcase and fanned a stack of documents. "Look at these papers." She made two stacks. "These show how sick he was and all the times he was in the hospital." She patted the second pile of papers while watching Heath to see how he reacted. "These are legal papers."

"Like the ones I had to sign for Uncle Hank."

"Right," Karen said, picking up the papers. "These show your father sued your mother."

Heath focused on Karen. "Why?"

A tear popped out before she could stop it. "So that he could see you."

"Really? Why didn't he just visit me?"

"You can find out by reading these papers, but from what I heard from him, your mother wouldn't let him. She claimed he was dangerous. Another time, the court said he could visit, but when he tried, he learned your mother had taken you away and hidden you somewhere. Later, when your father was in the hospital, he got a court order to force her to bring you to the hospital, but she never did. I was with him at that time so I know how hard he tried to see you."

Heath took the papers from Karen and held them to his chest as if they were precious. "My dad loved me, didn't he?"

"Yes he did."

Heath continued hugging the papers for a time before looking in the box again.

"What's this?" he asked looking at another card from the shoebox.

Karen took it and read it. "This is a prayer. It appears to be a prayer he wrote. From the looks of it, he probably held it often and read it over and over again." She scanned it quickly. "It's a prayer for you."

"What's it say?"

"I'll read it to you." Karen looked into Heath's eyes briefly before focusing on the card. "Dear God. Please watch over my son, Heath. I'm not going to be here to see that he's okay, but I know you will protect him. If I were here I would take him to church with me and help him become a Christian. My prayer is that someone else will do so." There were tears in Karen's eyes as she finished reading.

"I like that." Heath was silent for a few seconds. "Would you teach me to pray?"

"Do you know the Lord's Prayer?"

"I don't know any prayer."

"Well, we'll start with that. It's a comforting prayer. It goes like this:

Our Father, who art in heaven, hallowed be Thy name. Thy kingdom come, Thy will be done on earth as it is in heaven. Give us this day our daily bread. And forgive us our trespasses, as we forgive those who trespass against us. And lead us not into temptation, but deliver us from evil. For Thine is the kingdom, and the power, and the glory, forever.

"That is pretty," Heath said. "I like that. Comforting is the right word for it."

There was a knock on the door. "Yes?" she asked.

"Are you okay?" Richard asked through the closed door.

"Yes. We're fine."

"Cloris and Hank were wondering how much longer you're going to be in there."

Karen looked at Heath. He shrugged.

"We shouldn't be much longer," Karen said.

Heath spoke loudly. "Tell Mother I got everything I wanted, including a father who loved me. Tell her that."

"Okay. I'll tell her," Richard said.

"I like the prayer, but I don't understand it. I guess I need to go to church before it'll make sense to me. Would you help me with that? I don't want to make Mother mad, but I'm old enough to decide what I want to do. Dad said in his prayer for me that he hoped I would go to church, and, now that I know him, I want to do that."

Karen held back tears as she caught her breath. *Was this the reason, Lord?*

"That's right. You can make your own decision about going to church now. And I'd love to help. You can start by going with me."

"Okay. When?" Heath was smiling.

"This Sunday," she said.

They both stood. She turned to Heath and looked him in the eyes. "Is it okay if I hug you? You're my stepson, you know."

He tilted his head. "I am?"

"Yes. Is that okay?"

"Sure." He smiled, moved toward her with open arms, and they hugged.

After their embrace, Heath reached deep into his pants pocket and came out with his fist held out. "I have something for you, too. Open your hand."

She held out her hand to him and he dropped a gold ring in it. She picked it up to examine it more closely and saw that it was her Alpha Omega ring, the one she couldn't find in Bruges. She must have frowned.

"Oh, don't worry. I didn't steal it. I found it. Uncle Virgil had it and I knew it was yours so I sneaked it away from him."

"Uncle Virgil?"

"He's not really my uncle. He's my mother's boyfriend. I don't like him though."

"But he was in Europe with you?"

"Yes. Mother said that would be best."

"How'd you know it was my ring?"

"From those pictures I took of you at the wedding and in Germany. I blew one up on my laptop and that's when I saw you were wearing the ring with the funny letters on it."

She had given up on ever seeing that ring again. She hugged him again. "Thank you for keeping it for me."

"You're welcome."

"Now, before we get back to the lawyers and the mediator, what are we going to do about this case?" Karen asked.

"I don't know. I never meant to hurt you. Mother said it was the only way."

"Heath, how did you know how to find us in Germany?"

"Uncle Virgil knew. He'd been working for the head librarian, Liz, and found out all about your plans from her. You'll didn't show up when we thought you would , but we waited and then you came. We almost lost you when you went to Belgium, but Virgil is good at following people, and we jumped on the trains you took and bought the tickets once we were onboard."

"Why were you and Virgil in Germany and Belgium?"

"Mother said to take photos of your lavish living. She said we'd get more money from you with proof of your spending. I'm sorry I had to do that. I didn't mean you any harm. I sorta liked Germany, though. Virgil was there to help me since I'd never been anywhere without Mother."

"There was a fire at my house last night. Do you know about that?"

His eyes opened wide. "No, not really." He paused. "But Uncle Virgil smelled like smoke when he got home. I hope he didn't hurt anyone."

"Does he have a black pickup truck?"

"Yes. With tinted windows." Heath shook his head slowly. "He's a bad man. He talks nasty to my mother sometime."

"I think he's bad, too."

"He's going to go away, though."

"Why do you think that?" Karen asked.

"I heard him tell Mother last night that he was leaving the country for a while."

"Oh? What else did he say?"

"There was something about his pickup being sunk in town lake."

"You be careful around him," Karen said.

"Okay," Heath said.

"Well, we better get back to our rooms and finish this settling. Are you ready?"

"I guess," he said. "Will I see you again?"

"Of course. I thought you were going to church with me Sunday."

"You were serious about that?" He looked surprised.

"Yes. We're family. I was hoping you'd come spend the weekend. Do you like to fish?"

"I don't know." He paused a second before a huge grin popped out. "I bet I would like to fish."

"Good. We live on the water and you can fish right off the dock. You can come over Saturday and fish, then spend the night at my house and we'll go to church together."

"Wow," he said. "You're a great stepmother." He bounded out of the room.

After Heath left, Karen met with Richard and told him to submit a settlement offer to the opposing party. "Tell them we will pay one dollar and sign a statement saying we will not press charges against Cloris and Virgil for criminal activity."

To Richard's surprise, the settlement offer was quickly approved by Hank for Cloris and Heath and the lawsuit was over.

CHAPTER TWENTY-THREE

The lawsuit was settled and Brian didn't expect more trouble from the people who had sued Karen. So he didn't worry when she said she was going home, back to their place on Dry Creek. Even so, he ended his visit with his dad as soon as he could. Dad was released, though the damage had been heavy. He'd have to go to cardiac rehab, and would need some help for a while. Amy talked to her adviser and got permission to do most of her coursework online from California so she could stay with her grandfather until he recovered. Brian thanked Amy for her help, but he knew it wouldn't be his last trip to California. For now, though, he was ready to be with Karen again.

They had talked on the phone every day. She said she had a surprise for him, one she'd show him when he got home. Karen's actions no longer alarmed him. She could take care of herself. Even though he wanted to, he didn't need to be there to protect her. When she told him the whole story about getting out of the burning garage, dragging a suitcase of memories for Heath and a panicked Cathy, he realized he had nothing to be concerned about.

But there was more to it than that. It was in her voice. The confidence that had been missing since the day they got married. From other things she'd said, he suspected it was because she'd stuck with the lawsuit to learn what God had in store for her. In doing so, she learned why she'd been put into the situation—to lead her to a place where she once again trusted her instincts.

She sounded strong and happy. Self-assured and humble. She was the Karen he had fallen in love with thirty years ago and again last year.

He opened the front door and was surrounded by the smell of cooking bacon. It was four o'clock in the afternoon; late for breakfast. He walked into the kitchen and she stood in front of the range with a frying pan filled with scrambled eggs. The toaster sounded and two pieces of browned bread popped up. She turned off the burner, turned into his arms and held tight.

"Breakfast for dinner?" he asked when they came up for air.

"I've gotten off schedule with you gone," she said.

"I love breakfast anytime."

"This is for Heath," she said smiling. "But, don't worry, I made enough for you."

"Heath?" He glanced around. "He's here? Now?"

Karen nodded toward the dock. "He's fishing."

Brian saw him sitting on the dock holding a rod that looked a lot like one of Brian's. "Well, I'll be. Was this one of the conditions you agreed to in settling the case? You had to take the boy, huh?"

She laughed. "No. At least, not officially. It's just that we've gotten along great and he's asking questions about God. Do you know his mother never took him to church?"

"I can believe it. Remember, she's the one responsible for putting you in the hospital."

"Anyway, I invited Heath to spend the weekend and go to church with us tomorrow. I hope that's okay with you. He could use a father figure. I'm not sure I set up that rod and reel properly."

"Whatever you want is fine with me," he said. He hugged her again.

***

Karen loved it when Brian said that. It wasn't that he was weak and always giving in to her. He expressed his desires and needs, too. What he was saying was that he loved her and wanted her to be happy.

"Help me with these trays, Brian," she said. "We're eating on the dock. Orange juice?"

"That's good. I had coffee on the plane."

Brian picked up the tray filled with plates and utensils and glasses of orange juice while Karen took the tray of bacon, eggs and toast.

"I smell breakfast," Heath said as he stood, placed the rod on the dock and joined them at the table. He jumped when he saw Brian. "Oh, hi, Mr. Brian. I didn't know you were here."

Brian smiled. "I just got home." He placed the tray on the table and held out a hand to Heath. "Nice to see you again."

Heath smiled while shaking his hand. "You weren't so happy last time you saw me." The look on his face turned grave. "Miss Karen has forgiven me. I hope you will, too."

Karen could see Brian's eyes glaze over the way they did when he held back tears.

"Yes, Heath. I forgive you and I *am* happy to see you. You're welcome here anytime."

Brian grabbed plates and utensils for the three of them and placed them around the table. Heath saw what was going on and helped by giving each setting a glass of orange juice. "I love this stuff," he said, holding up a glass of the juice.

"Heath, did you wash your hands?"

Heath quickly wiped his hands on his pants. "No ma'am."

"Better do it. You probably have worm juice on them."

His eyes grew large and he ran into the kitchen.

Karen served each plate with scrambled eggs, bacon and toast. Brian went back to the kitchen for a jar of homemade jelly. When they sat, Heath grabbed a fork and started to dig in.

"Heath, would you mind if we bless the food first?" Karen asked.

"No, ma'am," he said with a big smile on his face.

Karen took Brian's hand and reached over to Heath who had a fork in his right hand. He held her hand with the fork sticking out at an awkward angle. Brian grabbed Heath's other hand.

Karen nodded to Brian.

"Dear God," Brian began, "thank you for this wonderful day and for our family. Thank you, too, for our special guest and watch over him and protect him. Bless this food. Amen."

Heath smiled. "I'm the special guest." His fork went to work.

"Yes you are," Karen said.

After dinner, Heath went back to fishing while Brian and Karen cleaned up. When they were done, they sat at the table on the dock with cups of hot tea and watched Heath while they talked.

"You didn't even notice," she said.

"Notice what?"

She dangled her right hand in front of him. "My ring."

His eyes popped open wider than she'd ever seen them. "Where did you get that?"

"From Heath."

"He's the one who took it?"

"No. He returned it. He said Virgil showed up with it in Bruges and Heath knew it was mine because he'd seen it on my hand in a photo he took in Hildesheim."

"No kidding."

"Yes. He swiped it from Virgil to return it to me."

"I didn't think we'd ever see that ring again."

"Me neither." Karen took Brian's hand and held it close. "Do you know this is the happiest day of my life?"

Brian looked at her and smiled. "Well, that's good to hear. You deserve to be happy."

"Thank you," she said. "And I want to tell you I'm sorry for the way I've been since the lawsuit was filed. You were probably asking why you'd married such a crazy person."

"No, never," he said, shaking his head.

"You're just being nice, but I know you were worried about me for a while. To tell the truth, I was worried myself. It wasn't easy for me either, but I learned God uses us when we go where we're most uncomfortable. Whether you believe it was worth it or not, our marriage is stronger now because of the lawsuit. Because I'm stronger."

"Then it was worth it," Brian said. Heath was at the end of the pier, far enough away so he couldn't hear them, but Brian lowered his voice anyway. "Tell me the latest with the lawsuit. I know you settled the case and had to pay a whopping sum of one dollar to Cloris. Have you heard what's going to happen to her?"

Karen shook her head. "I'm not sure what the police will do with the information we've given them, but I'm not going to press charges. To be honest, I don't want to do anything to hurt Heath. With Virgil gone, I think she'll do better. Heath said he'd never seen her drunk until Virgil showed up. I think Virgil conned her the same way he did Liz. Cloris needs help, not jail. Richard is pushing for counseling for her."

"Good," he said. "Heath is old enough to get out on his own and I think that would be good for him. I don't think he was allowed to mature. It seems like his mother purposely kept him dependent on her. Let me know if I can help. Like you said, he could use a father figure. Did he finish high school? Does he want to go to college. Does he have a job? We can help with all that."

"Good questions," Karen said. "I hoped you might offer to help."

"What about Cloris's lawyer brother? What's his name?"

"Hank Unger."

"Yeah. You said he pulled some pretty dirty tricks in the courthouse. Any of them illegal?"

"I don't think so," Karen said, "Remember, this was his first case after being admitted to the bar. Richard filed a complaint against him for one incident of ethics, but he thinks the bar will go easy on him this time."

"Virgil seems to be the culprit here, and he disappeared." Brian shook his head.

"Heath said he'd overheard Virgil tell his mother he was going to leave the country. What about Liz? Have you heard how she's doing since she learned about Virgil's background?"

"I talked to her several times while I was in California, mostly about library business. The one time I asked she said she was okay. She hasn't said anything else about Virgil to me, and I was reluctant to bring it up again. I asked Tex if he'd heard anything, and he let me know that even though she's a forgiving person, she's made an exception in Virgil's case. Tex said she probably hadn't let anyone get close to her like that since her husband died."

"That's a shame," Karen said. "She's such a wonderful person. I hope she finds the right man someday. She deserves a little happiness."

"Tex said the police found Virgil's truck. Seems the water wasn't deep enough to cover the top at the place in the lake were he dumped it. A jogger saw it and called 911 thinking there might be someone in the cab. Turns out the truck was leased in Cloris's name. She denies knowing anything about it. I tend to believe her on this one, based on the way Virgil was able to con Liz."

"Me, too," Karen said.

They watched Heath fish for a few minutes.

Karen broke the silence. "I'm glad the case has been settled. I never once thought it would end up this way, with Heath here visiting us like he is. All he wanted was to learn more about his father."

"How do you feel about him being here?"

"I am amazed. Do you realize God's love lives on from Ernest to Heath? And, I got to be the intermediary. There's no telling what this will lead to. And it's all because of his father's letters that sat forgotten in my attic for two decades."

"Yes. That is definitely amazing. Oh, I forgot to tell you. Ron called and said the bookmobile is ready to go. He said the paint job made it look like new."

"I guess we'll be back to work Monday," she said.

"Maybe," Brian said. "We need to talk about that."

"Why?"

"Liz said she is ready to buy one for the library."

"So? Liz also said Austin is big enough for two bookmobiles. That means we have the option of continuing if we want to."

"Do you?" Brian asked.

Karen looked into his eyes. "I've been thinking about whether or not we should move."

"Move?" he asked. "I thought you liked it here."

"I do. And I like my place in Sunset Valley." But that's just it. This is your place and that's my place. I'm suggesting a new place."

"A neutral place?"

"Yes. Actually, a retirement community."

Brian looked at her like she'd lost her mind. "What are you talking about? Where?"

"Not far from here. Georgetown. A place called Sun City, Texas."

Brian's eyes widened. "Sun City? Isn't that for old people?"

She laughed. "Guess what? In case you haven't noticed, we're eligible to live there. You only have to be fifty-five. I don't call that old. Do you? What I like about it is all the activities they have.

"But we'd have to move to Georgetown," he said.

"That's not far. We'd be close enough to Austin to see our friends and go to events there any time we wanted to."

"And to watch over Heath occasionally."

Heath cast his line and almost fell into the creek. After he regained his footing, he turned to them and waved.

"Uhh. He may need closer supervision for a while. If we do move, maybe he could stay with us in Georgetown until he's strong enough to get out on his own."

"If that's what you want we'll drive up there sometime and look around."

"I'm glad you feel that way," she said. "I reserved us a three-night stay in their vacation get-away village for next weekend. They'll give us a full tour of the place. And you know what else? I think they could use a bookmobile there."

Brian smiled. "Well, you sound like you're serious about this place. Hmm. I did promise to grow old with you."

They stood and embraced.

"I love you," she said.

"I love you, too. There's no cliffs to roll down in Sun City are there?"

"We'll see."

ACKNOWLEDGEMENTS

Writing a book, especially a book of fiction, can be a lonely job. However, as soon as I finish the first draft, I realize it is impossible to complete a book without the help of many people.

I would like to thank my wife Celeste for reading the first draft of *Love Lives On* and letting me know it is indeed a novel and not merely the ramblings of a writer. Her comments and suggestions were incorporated, resulting in major improvements to the story. My friends Rollo and Sylvia Newsom read an early draft and concurred with Celeste and added more suggestions which improved the story even more.

Next, I would like to thank my editor, Lisa Lickel. As an author of Christian fiction she was able to suggest many ways to improve the story and make it more fun to read. I was looking for someone to correct my grammar and she gave me much more. She gave me a better book.

While Lisa made her final pass, checking my changes, I sent advanced review copies to my friends Mary Cates, Peg Case, Jim Chapman, Joy Hannabass, Joyce Joiner, Kimberly Martin, and Laura North. I would like to think them all for taking the time to read the book and for their comments and suggestions. Some very important changes resulted from their effort, changes that will make the book more enjoyable for future readers.

Other contributors include Lorri S. Ramey and Kendra R. LaLonde, plus the dozens of friends who commented on cover designs.

In addition to the people named above, I benefited from participating with the following organizations: The John 3:16 Marketing Network, American Christian Fiction Writers, especially the CenTex Chapter, San Gabriel Writers' League, and the Central Texas Authors.

ABOUT THE AUTHOR

Sidney W. Frost is a former Stephen Minister, and a member of his church choir at First United Methodist Church in Georgetown, Texas. He has served on the session at a Presbyterian church, and has been on the vestry at several Episcopal churches.

While singing with the Austin Lyric Opera Chorus, he was in 42 productions. He and his wife, Celeste, sing with the San Gabriel Chorale and have been in several Berkshire Festivals.

Until May, 2010, he was an Adjunct Professor at Austin Community College where he taught computer courses. He received the adjunct teaching excellence award in 2005.

While attending the University of Texas in the 1960's he worked part-time at the Austin Public Library driving a bookmobile after completing service in the U.S. Marines. His first novel idea involved a bookmobile librarian and, although that book was never completed, he has included the librarian and the bookmobile in all his books.

He is an active member of the American Christian Fiction Writers and the San Gabriel Writers' League.

He has a Master of Science degree from the University of Houston and a Bachelor of Arts from the University of California at Long Beach.

Awards for his first novel, *Where Love Once Lived*, include First Place in the 2007 SouthWest Writers Contest, First Place in the 2007 Writers' League of Texas Novel Manuscript Contest, Third Place in the Fourteenth Annual Lone Star Writing Competition, Northwest Houston Chapter of the Romance Writers of America, and Finalist in the 2006 Yosemite Writers Contest.

The Vengeance Squad (Kindle edition) has been a bestseller on Amazon.com in the Religious Mystery category.

AUTHOR INTERVIEW

Q: When did you first know that you would be an author?

My earliest memory of writing is when my older sister, Barbara Cagle, decided we would publish a neighborhood magazine. We were living on Pete's Path in Austin, Texas at the time, so I had to be about twelve years old.

By "publish," keep in mind the magazine was handwritten and each copy was copied by hand as well. So there wasn't a wide distribution and the magazine only lasted for a summer. When school started we were too busy to continue it.

It wasn't until much later that I had that feeling I think all writers must get that boils down to a need to create something. I started several novels, wrote short stories, had a newspaper column for a while, and was assigned writing projects at various jobs throughout my career in computing.

Q: Who are your favorite authors?

My all-time favorite author is James Michener. I love the way he researched and described a geographical area so that it came alive. My favorite authors of Christian fiction are Jan Karon, Dee Henderson, and Philip Gulley. I review books for several publishers and belong to a neighborhood book club so I read a variety of books by many authors.

Q: Share with us your journey to publication.

The idea for writing *Where Love Once Lived* came to me while driving a bookmobile back in the 1960s. I was a college student at the University of Texas assigned to drive for a feisty librarian who got us into trouble with the head librarian several times because of helping our patrons in ways unrelated to books.

The nudge to write the bookmobile story came again in 2004, and this time I said no because I knew it was too hard. The very next Sunday, my pastor, Dr. Jeanie Stanley, said this: "Trust the Lord God with your dreams and he will help you achieve them." Four years later I had a good start for what eventually became *Where Love Once Lived*.

Q: What advice do you have for aspiring authors?

I am often asked how one goes about writing a novel and getting it published. All I can tell them is about my own experience. However, I can add where I made mistakes so they can skip some of the trial and error I went through. For example, one thing I learned too late was that you should know the market before you start writing.

Another thing I tell people is to take classes. Not just for what you learn from instructors, but for what you learn from reading your classmates' work and what they say about yours.

AFTERWORD

Thank you for reading *Love Lives On*. If you haven't already, I hope you will read *Where Love Once Lived* and *The Vengeance Squad*. See my website, http://sidneywfrost.com, for the latest information about all my books.

You may also want to visit the Christian Bookmobile:

http://christianbookmobile.blogspot.com/

This is where I talk about writing, review books, interview other Christian authors and occasionally talk about growing up in Austin, Texas.

I also respond to e-mail queries and would love to hear from you: sidfrost@suddenlink.net.

WHERE LOVE ONCE LIVED
CHAPTER ONE

Karen felt loved on Tuesdays.

She was fifty-three and divorced with a college-aged daughter at home who'd probably flee the nest soon, leaving Karen to live alone. She'd missed her chance for happiness. Still, she wasn't sad. Teaching and her volunteer work as a lay minister, hospital chaplain, and member of her church choir fulfilled her. To be honest, she wanted more. She wanted the special kind of love she felt on Tuesdays.

She glanced at the clock on the wall as the familiar knock sounded. The third graders snapped to attention, turning their heads in unison toward the door. Today was the day. Every Tuesday about this time for the past six weeks, a fresh bouquet of flowers arrived. Karen opened the door and felt a rush of warmth when she realized today would be no exception.

Peeking around the blooms with his usual grin, his black curls poking out from under the well-worn blue cap that sat too far back on his head, the deliveryman thrust the vase toward her.

"Morning, Ms. Williams."

"Good morning, Sam. It must be Tuesday." She took the flowers, admiring this week's selection of red roses. Her friend, Cathy, warned her to be cautious because the flowers might be from a stalker, but Karen didn't think so.

"Yes, ma'am, 'tis."

Sam wasn't much for words, but his facial expressions said it all. He knew something she didn't know, and his eyes bragged about it.

"You can't tell me who's sending these, right?"

The scent of the roses overpowered the usual classroom odor. Without the flowers, her room smelled like a combination of peanut butter and floor cleaner.

"Nope." After he said it, he pursed his lips as if to hold in his secret.

Karen imagined the Tuesday delivery was a highlight for Sam because of the way he acted each week. She didn't want to disappoint him today.

"Don't know or can't say?"

"Can't say." He turned to leave, but suddenly spun around. "And don't know." His eyes sparkled as he backed out of the room, keeping his gaze on her all the while.

After Sam shut the door, she held the bouquet for the class to see. Let the children make their jokes so they could get back to the lesson. Nine year olds loved distractions, but they enjoyed this mystery most of all because it involved their teacher. The student teacher, Fran Rush, sitting at the back of the classroom, smiled and shook her head as if she knew what was coming next.

"Who are the flowers from, Ms. Williams?" Jose asked.

"Well, let's see." She placed the vase on her desk and pulled out the card, repeating the weekly ritual. As usual, all it said was, "To Karen, with love." She peeked over the card to watch Jose's response as she continued. "Oh, no. It's not signed."

"Again?" Haley asked, playing along.

Jose pumped his hand high in the air, his eyes opened wide. "I know! I know! It's from your secret a'mirer."

Karen couldn't guess who that might be or why the flowers came on Tuesdays, for that matter. Could it be Leon? He'd asked her out once, but she turned him down and never encouraged him. Besides, Leon wasn't the type to do something in secret. He'd be bragging about it to everyone in the church choir.

As she wondered about the mystery, Karen peered out the window at the florist's delivery van in the school parking lot in time to see it leaving. As it disappeared behind the administration building, another vehicle came into view, one that looked like a bus with no windows. On its side in large letters was Austin Public Library Bookmobile.

She'd once loved a bookmobile driver. Memories of that time with him poured in so rapidly she caught her breath. It'd been long ago, but her heart remembered. At first she thought of the love she'd felt back then, but the good memories didn't last long. She'd gone to the bookmobile as usual that last day, but nothing was to be the same again. She went to Brian with love and exciting news. She left alone. Not just without him, but alone in the world and apart from God.

This couldn't be the same bookmobile. Nevertheless, she had to see it. She had to walk into it and face her fears. She grabbed her jacket to shield her from the damp November day and rounded up her class.

"Get your coats on, kids. We're going to the library."

The children grumbled at the notion, but when they saw what kind of library it was, they stepped livelier. Karen walked inside the bookmobile after making sure Miss Rush had control of the children. She inhaled the familiar odor of used books. She traveled back thirty years with a single whiff. The librarian just inside the front door welcomed her with a smile. A man sat at a desk near the back of the vehicle. Karen pulled a book off the shelf and held it next to her chest, not caring what the title was. With her eyes closed, she could feel Brian standing next to her, loving her, and it was so real, she felt her eyes moisten.

Enough. That was too long ago. She dabbed her eyes and looked around. Fran was up front letting the children in a few at a time. "Fran, will you watch the children? I'm going to the room."

Fran nodded in a way that said she'd seen Karen's tears and was concerned. Explanations would be needed, but not now.

When Karen reached the back door, she gasped and froze. He wasn't supposed to be here.

"Brian?" she asked.

He looked more like a professor than the student she'd known in college. His blue eyes sparkled, and she recognized his smile at once. The neatly trimmed beard was new, but it didn't hide the strong jawline she'd once loved.

He jumped to his feet and moved toward her with his arms open. "Hello, Karen. I knew you'd come."

His movement frightened her, but there was nowhere to run. She blocked the embrace he was heading for by taking his hands in hers and pretending to want to shake hands.

"What are you doing here?" She was composed on the outside, but the rhythm of her heartbeat told her she was anything but calm. "I thought you were in California." She dropped his hands and pushed away, putting as much distance between them as possible in the cramped quarters of the mobile library.

"I was, but I moved to Austin about six months ago."

"Mister?" asked a piping voice.

"What's up, Haley?" Karen asked the student who was peeking up at Brian.

Haley pointed to the woman sitting near the front door. "She told me to ask the man where to find the biographies."

Brian moved to the shelves on his left and knelt eye to eye with Haley. "They're right here, young lady."

She loved the way he focused on her student, but knew she should get away now before she said something she'd regret. He'd hurt her in a way she couldn't easily forgive.

Then she saw the ring. On his right hand was the wide gold band with the Greek letters Alpha and Omega, the beginning and the end. She knew there was a date engraved inside that marked the start of their life together. She knew it was there because she had a matching ring in her jewelry box. A relic of the past she couldn't bear to toss when she'd married Steve.

"I've worn it ever since you gave it to me," he said as he stood and moved toward her.

Could he still read her mind, or had she focused on his hand a bit too long? She peered into his eyes, as blue as his shirt, and ignored what he said. "I see you have your old job back."

He laughed. "I tried, but the city doesn't have bookmobiles anymore. I had to buy this one myself."

His laugh. She remembered that, too, and it took her back to a pleasant time of her life. Their two-year relationship was with laughter. Even so, it ended with sadness so deep there was little laughter for Karen for years afterward.

"Why did you buy a bookmobile?"

He shrugged. "Looking for happiness, I guess. I'm not sure it was because of the job or because it was the time when you were in my life." He moved closer and gazed into her eyes as if waiting for a response.

She felt the heat of his body and smelled his familiar scent, both so strong she turned away. The last time she saw him was in a bookmobile long ago when they were students at the University of Texas. That was the day he broke up with her and left her alone. She didn't want to think about that day. She walked as far to the rear of the vehicle as possible, motioning him to follow.

When they were near the back door, she stood close to him so the children couldn't hear her voice. She felt her body shiver. "Why are you here? Why are you doing this?"

"Because of you," he said and smiled.

For years, she knew what she'd say if their paths ever crossed. She even rehearsed it from time to time for the first few years they were apart. Too many years had passed for that speech. All she wanted to do now was to find out what was going on and leave. A thought came to her.

"Did you send the flowers?"

"Yes," he said. "Did you like them?"

"Don't send any more." The secret admirer dream burst, or rather fizzled. "I still don't understand why you bought a bookmobile."

He beamed. "You should know."

An image leaped into her head. This time it wasn't one of the day he said goodbye. She remembered a time before that when they were alone in the bookmobile. It was a time when his lips were on hers as she leaned against a bookshelf. For a split second, it was as if they were still there, still in love, still touching.

"All I remember is your dumping me in a vehicle like this."

He grimaced then looked her eyes. "I'm sorry. I was thinking about a different time. I never wanted to break up with you."

She wanted to forgive him for everything and move into his arms where she once felt so safe and loved. Instead, she stared at him, waiting, listening. He'd never told her why he'd left her, and her pride had kept her from telling him her news. It was too late.

His eyes focused on hers, and his voice comforted her with his sincerity. "I knew you wouldn't want to see me again. That's why I bought this bookmobile. I wanted to make you curious enough to come in."

Sunlight streamed in through the door window, highlighting new wrinkles around his eyes. She remembered his birthday. He was fifty-four, more handsome than when they'd first met so long ago.

"It worked. You got me to come in, but don't count on seeing me again. Goodbye."

She went out the door without looking back, finding it easy to resist the urge to forgive him.

***

Brian had planned this reunion for months after dreaming about it for years. He'd considered a multitude of possible reactions on Karen's part, but he hadn't expected her to walk away before he could tell her why he had broken up with her. If she would hear him out, she'd forgive him. After that, anything was possible. He had to stop her.

"Liz," he hollered toward the front of the bookmobile, "I'll be back."

He ran to catch up to Karen. "Please wait. Let me explain."

She was halfway to the school building when she stopped and turned toward him. "Why?" Her voice was stronger now, but her eyes were moist.

He hadn't counted on the tears. He'd hurt her enough for a lifetime and didn't want to see her in pain, but he felt he had to continue. "I know you're angry, but please let me tell you what happened."

She was silent. Could it be his long journey home would end like this? She had the power to extinguish the hope he'd carried for so long. He would've come back sooner if it hadn't been for his daughter. Was it too late?

"Okay, I'll listen. But just long enough for you to tell me why you walked out on me the way you did." She pulled back the left sleeve of her jacket and glanced at her watch.

This wasn't the way it was supposed to be. The reunion he'd dreamed of had them sitting together in front of a warm fireplace. He had his arm around her, and she looked at him lovingly, chin upraised slightly, ready and waiting for his kiss. Here they were standing in a parking lot outside an elementary school, and he was on the clock. He almost prayed for help before he remembered God had forsaken him. All he could do was hope honesty was enough.

"It happened when I went back to my parents' home for the holidays. That trip I took before we split up. I didn't want to go, but Mother begged me to. She wanted the whole family home for Christmas. I was so in love with you, all I could think about was our future together. I left here vowing by the next Christmas, we'd never be separated again."

"So, what happened?" Karen's voice was monotone and her face expressionless.

He'd never told anyone what he was about to tell her, not even his best friend. Phil probably guessed what happened, but he'd never brought it up.

"When I got to Redondo, a girl I knew in high school invited me out. It seemed okay at the time because it wasn't a date and she wasn't anyone special to me. It was like a reunion with a classmate, talking about old times."

Karen crossed her arms. He felt her tenseness and wanted to wrap his arms around her and comfort her.

"I still don't know how things went beyond that. Up until that time, I always thought of myself as an honest, moral person. If there's a God, I was tested and failed."

She raised both hands with palms down. "Look. You don't have to say anymore."

"Please. I need to tell you everything. I need your forgiveness."

When she dropped her arms, he continued. "I can't justify what happened next. I've often wondered why I did it. It was stupid, and I'll always regret it. Before I knew what happened she was pregnant, and she assumed I would marry her to give the baby a name. I never loved her, and she never loved me."

"You stayed married?"

"Yes. We raised our daughter together. Otherwise, we lived separate lives. I immersed myself in my work and she in her social life. As soon as Amy was grown, I filed for divorce."

"Where is your daughter now?" Karen asked.

"She lives in Redondo Beach, not far from where I grew up. Raising her kept me sane. We're very close." He heard children behind him and looked back to see Karen's class walking toward them with the other teacher. His time with Karen was ending. He'd told her the truth. Was it enough?

She sighed. Not a sigh of relief, but one associated with an onerous task.

"Thank you." Karen's voice softened. "I saw the pain in your face as you spoke, and I know it wasn't easy for you to tell me what happened." She paused and cleared her voice before continuing. "I'm just sorry you made your decision about marrying without discussing it with me at the time. I could've helped if you'd confided in me."

He loved the sound of her voice, but didn't understand her words. "What do you mean? I had to do the right thing. I had no choice."

"You had choices," she said. "You were my first love, the first person I trusted with my deepest feelings." Her head bent forward

slightly as she swallowed, and Brian saw new tears forming. "And you broke my heart."

Her words hurt, but no more than the ones he'd said to himself over the years.

"But—"

"Wait." Her eyes pierced through the film of tears. "I listened to you. Now, you listen to me. I loved you then, and I knew you loved me. We had something special, and I, too, had begun to think about future Christmases together. Think how shocked I was when you broke it off without an explanation. Then later, when I learned you were married, I thought you must have been dating both of us at the same time, and I wasn't as important to you as I'd believed."

"I loved you. Only you." He moved toward her, wanting to take her in his arms and show his love. "Karen, I...."

She pushed him away. "You had a funny way of showing your love. Now, here you are, back in town with flowers and a bookmobile and your fancy words of remorse. I suppose you want to pick up where we left off."

She was mocking him, but he didn't care. "Yes."

"Alright then," she said with a strong voice. She pushed her open jacket away and placed her hands on her hips. "Where we left off was at the point where I didn't care for you at all. Nothing has changed." She turned toward the school.

He'd expected her to be mad about the way he'd broken up with her, but she was angrier than he thought she'd be, especially after so many years.

"Can't we back up to where you said you loved me?"

"Impossible." She shook her head. "Too much happened after that." She joined the students when they reached the place where Brian and Karen stood, and she walked with them toward the school building.

"How about meeting after school?" he asked. "We need more time to talk."

She continued walking away. "There's no reason to talk more. And stop sending the flowers."

"Is he your secret a'mirer, Ms. Williams?" a student asked.

"Don't talk, Haley," Karen said.

"Think about the good times we had together," Brian said. The children giggled. He didn't care.

He stood in the parking lot until she disappeared into the classroom and the door closed behind her. When he turned to go back to the bookmobile, he saw Liz standing in the door, watching him.